DATO

T.S. Wieland

Read more books by T.S. Wieland at

www.TSWieland.com
or
www.SemAdventures.com

DATO is a work of fiction. Characters, locations, and names are all based on either events, people, or locations, or are a product of the author's imagination, or are used fictitiously. Any resemblance to actual persons, living or dead, events, or locales is entirely coincidental.

DATO. Copyright © by T.S. Wieland. All rights reserved. No print of this book may be used or reproduced in any way without written permission except in the case of brief quotations embodied in critical articles and reviews.

Written by TS Wieland
Cover Design by Tey Bartolome
Edited by Loring Wirbel, Christy Gravitt, and Tammie Wieland

SECOND EDITION

ISBN-13: 978-0-9991941-2-6
ISBN-10: 0-9991941-2-7

Writer's Forethought

Humanity has come to define itself by the massive number of achievements made over thousands of years, by the obstacles needed to be overcome by our sheer human will to survive. We measure our success by our ability to work in groups to survive the harsh winters or inventing new methods to provide energy to every home. It is our ability to survive when the odds are against us and succeed when we were almost destined to fail, that makes up who we are as a species.

Many of these accomplishments are known throughout the world, while some have gone unsung. Others have been lost to the sands of time. The purpose of this novel is pay tribute to those both praised and unsung heroes. Those who never gave up when all hope was lost. Those who endured the unimaginable.

Deriving from classic survival tales of human perseverance, this story explores the problem-solving skills of the human mind, as well as its terrifying capabilities when pushed to the very limits. It is a memento of humanities effortless need to broaden our horizons and explore vast deserts with no regard for safety or comfort. This struggle is presented as an adventurous horror story of both monsters and men, and the blurred boundary between them. It is not a joyful or happy tale, but one of pain and heartbreak meant to acknowledge the often unrecognized and untapped capabilities of humanity.

Prologue

May 30, 2187
- Earth Station 11 -

*K*nock! Knock! Knock!

The commander reached over in the darkness from the comfort of his bed for the light switch on his night stand. The lights turned on to a low dim. He sat up in his bed and coughed to himself, trying to clear his throat.

Knock! Knock! Knock! The knocking on the door continued.

"One minute!" shouted the commander at the door. He reached down and picked his pants up off the floor and began to slip them on. He looked over at his clock. It was two twenty-nine in the morning by standard station time. He huffed with disgust.

Knock! Knock! Knock!

"I said give me a minute!" shouted the commander once more. "Whoever you are."

The commander grabbed his glasses from off the nightstand and shuffled over to the door. He pressed his hand on the door button, watching it slide open and reveal who had disturbed his sleep.

"Commander, I'm so sorry for waking you," said the newest employee, Russell, sounding rather distressed and urgent.

"Russell, I've told you everything you need to know. You're a bright kid, and I'm sure whatever the problem is, you'll figure it out. Life will go on," replied the commander. He started to walk away from the door.

"No, sir. It's not that. We just..." replied Russell fumbling through his words. Russell's ability in taking initiative wasn't his strong suit. His first two stressful weeks as the newest station operator were about to become even more stressful.

"It's just what, Russell?" the commander replied with a sigh.

"We... I mean there's-"

"I'm not going to play twenty questions with you, Russell. You either tell me what's wrong, or I'm going back to sleep."

"There's a ship coming in, sir!"

"Yes, this is a docking station, Russell. There are always ships coming in," the commander replied with a sarcastic tone.

"No, the ship, it's not responding, sir!"

"What do you mean? Did you hail it?" replied the commander now looking rather concerned.

"Yes, sir. But there is no response. We've been trying to get into contact with them for the past fifteen minutes."

The commander pushed past Russell and made his way down the residency hall behind him. Russell turned around and immediately began following. The commander marched his way down the hall to the main control room, hoping the captain of the possible ghost ship had either stepped away for a moment or had only lost radio transmission. He reached into his pocket and realized he didn't have his key card, letting out an irritated grunt.

"I've got it, sir," said Russell running over to him.

Russell fumbled with his key, making sure it was turned the correct way. The commander waited impatiently. Russell swiped his key card across the door. The commander hastily pushed the sliding door aside and made his way up the steps to the console.

Ahead of the commander, through the series of windows spanning the control deck, was a complete view of the station docking bay, floating elegantly in the darkness of space as the station spun slowly in its fixed orbit around the Earth. Each airlock, hangar and docking module could be seen from the main deck window, and only two ships were currently docked with the station out of six hangars available.

"Is it not on the list?" asked the commander of his communications officer, Zac.

"No, she's on the docking schedule. She's just not slowing down and there is no response from the crew. We received a message from the last station she just came from informing us they received a distress signal from her. They sent back a reply, but the ship went dark after that," said Zac listening to his headphones.

"Try them again," said the commander.

"Space vessel DATO Six, this is Earth Station Eleven. Do you copy? Over," asked Zac into his headset.

Zac pressed the speaker button on the console in front of him so everyone could hear the ship's response. Russell stood next to the commander as all three of them listened to the static over the speaker. There was no reply from the ship.

"What's their course?" asked the commander.

"They are currently on a collision course with station eight. Seventy-nine thousand meters per second and holding, sir." Zac replied.

"Jesus, they're coming in at full speed!" exclaimed the commander staring out at the window. "Try them again! Russell, hail station eight and let them know we have a runaway on a direct collision course with them!"

Russell swiftly sat down in his chair and picked up his headset.

"Space vessel DATO Six, this is Earth Station Eleven. You are on a direct collision course. You are instructed to reduce your speed immediately and alter your course," said Zac into his microphone.

The static continued for a moment, followed by a brief broken message. "St-…, is-…, ver-…,"

A moment of silence passed. "Wa-…, ort-…, shot-… So-…, tion-…, ven-…, vance-…."

Watching Russell fumble through the controls, Zac reached across and pushed the station call button for him, shaking his head at his co-workers' inexperience. The commander stepped over toward the window, trying to get a glimpse of the incoming ship. DATO Six was just a small speck out the viewport window, a white shimmering point in the blackness of space.

Russell waited for the response from the station on his headset. "This is station eight," replied a female operator voice.

"Uh-Station eight, hey, this is station eleven. We have a runaway ship on a collision course with your station," said Russell jumping right to the point.

The commander turned around and looked at Russell over the console. "Tell them to begin evacuation immediately!"

Russell nodded to him.

The commander looked back out the window to see the amber lights to the station begin to flash. The station had begun its evacuation. The commander only hoped they weren't too late.

"She's starting to reduce speed, commander," said Zac, looking at the console.

"Have they responded?" asked the commander.

"No. Still no reply."

"They've begun evacuations, uh-sir!" said Russell.

"Contact every ship in our sector and have them divert their orbits away from this sector until further notice," said the commander back to Russell.

"Uh, how sir?" asked Russell.

The commander hurried back around the console. He tapped on the computer screen, showing the map of all the ships in the area waiting in orbit. "Call each one labeled SC11."

The evacuation pods from the station sprang from the exterior one by one and began their descent toward the Earth below. A bright flash caught everyone's attention out the window in the distance. They all looked up to see the incoming ship burst into flames.

The room fell silent.

They all stared out the window, watching silently.

The flames dispersed, revealing that the ship was still intact and continuing its collision course toward the station.

"Russell!" shouted the commander back over to him.

"Right away, sir!" Russell replied turning back to his computer.

Zac looked back down at his console.

"They are slowing down, sir!"

"What? How? Will they slow down before they reach the station?" asked the commander.

"No, they are at fifty-eight meters per second, sir, and dropping."

Another bright flash came from out over the horizon. Everyone looked out the window again as the explosion quickly faded.

"She's at forty-seven meters now, and dropping," said Zac looking at the computer.

The commander stepped over to the window once more. The small explosions on the horizon were now growing bigger and brighter as they approached, each one flaring up from the bow of the ship.

"Thirty-six meters," bellowed Zac.

Another explosion flared from the incoming vessel.

"Twenty-nine meters."

"How are they slowing down?" asked Russell looking up at the window.

The commander stepped forward and stared out the window.

"Their oxygen. They are blowing up their oxygen reserves to try and reduce their speed. Their engines must be damaged, as well as their communications," said the commander, watching another explosion.

Zac and Russell looked up away from their consoles, mesmerized.

"Nine thousand meters per second!" shouted Zac, looking back down.

Russell stood up from his chair and stared out the window, as another explosion engulfed the ship. He glanced over at Station Eight out the window, seeing there were only a few evacuation pods left.

"Four thousand meters!"

The whole ship could now be made out. The bow of the ship appeared almost nonexistent, with a massive gaping hole in the front.

"Eight hundred meters!"

Zac stood up from his console and looked out at the ship as it approached. They all watched the ship grow larger and larger as it approached, still moving way too fast to even attempt docking with any of the stations.

As the massive ship barreled its way toward them, they could all see the front of the ship leaking oxygen from the bow to try and reduce speed, followed by another brighter and closer explosion.

Close enough now to see into the bridge's shattered observation window, a single pilot in a space suit sat at the command console with a lowered sun visor. The pilot's appearance was then lost in the reflection off the windows.

A single escape pod jettisoned from the damaged vessel as it approached, steering its way past the space station window before beginning its gradual descent down to Earth.

DATO

    The ship careened passed the station's window, uncomfortably close. The commander gazed out at the broken vessel as it passed, seeing the large gaping wound in the ship's hull which stretched the full length of the mid ship, all the way up to the bridge, exposing the ship's interior to the lifeless vacuum of space.

    The ship collided with the two hangars from the now presumably abandoned space station in a cataclysmic, silent explosion.

    The crew of Earth Station Eleven stood idle in awe watching the all but destroyed vessel make its final plunge toward the Earth.

One

DATO 6
- En Route to Doris Station -
(30 Days Earlier)

    Lara laid on her back under the small Schooner spacecraft, using a pair of wire cutters to clean the singed ends off the copper wires in her right hand. Her boots were sticking out from under the spacecraft, with her music playing in the background on the docking bay speakers.

    "All right, little man. Let's not have a repeat of last time," she said to herself.

    She reached up into the open panel and clipped the first wire into the open electrical port. She took a deep breath, reaching up to carefully attach the last wire.

    "Lara!" shouted a male voice loudly over the ship's intercom.

    Lara jumped, brushing the wire ends against the connectors, showering her in a rain of sparks.

    "Shit!" she yelled, banging her fist against the bottom of the spacecraft.

"Please report to the bridge," said the voice calmly.

Lara laid her head back down on the metal Schooner bay floor. She grabbed the flashlight next to her and pointed it into the small port to see the damage. She had successfully shorted to the connectors, and would now have to replace them all once again.

She let out an aggravated sigh.

Resting the flashlight down on the floor, she sluggishly crawled her way out from under the spacecraft. Wiping her hands off on her dirty jumpsuit, she walked over to the elevator and pressed the call button. She waited impatiently for the elevator, rubbing her fingers across her bracelet made from a woven elastic string, with a plastic hospital ID tag attached to it, to try and ease her frustration.

The glass doors to the elevator opened. Lara stepped inside and tapped the main deck button on the digital display. The elevator moved backward through the ship, stopped at the mid ship elevator shaft and ascended to the bridge.

The elevator doors opened. Lara stepped out and began her march toward the bridge, down the long white and navy blue painted hallway lined with doors on her left side, and a long glass overlook out into the dark void of space on her right. She stopped at the bridge airlock, entered her code, and waited for the four corners of the doorway to unlock before opening.

Stepping onto the bridge, she could see Artie resting with his feet up on the console while leaning back in his chair, gazing out at the asteroid belt ahead rotating from the ship's gravitational spin.

"What the hell, Art!?" she roared at him.

"You almost done fixing the defroster?" he asked her, still looking out the window.

"Are you serious?! I was until you ruined everything!"

"Yea, I saw," Artie replied lowering his feet to the ground. "You enjoy your meteor shower under there?"

Artie swiveled his chair around and smiled at her through his beige beard, gazing at his wife, her jumpsuit covered in grease stains, her dark brown and faded highlighted hair a tussled mess.

Lara looked at the video feed from the hangar bay on his control panel with her amber colored eyes, seeing the Schooner plainly in view replaying the infuriating moment repeatedly. "You were watching me rather than helping me the whole time?"

Artie shrugged. "You looked like you had everything under control."

Lara glared at him with her murky green eyes, grinding her teeth under her lips. Artie smiled back at her scowling gaze with a smug expression. "We're less than seventeen hours away, so you'd best get it fixed before we need to dock."

"Or you can just hang outside and clean the windshield for Pat," Lara replied. She turned around and started walking away.

Artie reached out and grabbed her by the hand to drag her back over to him. He tugged her back over to his chair, forcing her to sit in his lap. "Come here. I'm sorry I almost got you electrocuted."

Lara laid back in his lap with her legs over the armrest, trying not to make eye contact with him. She often loathed her husband's shenanigans and childish games. Although she secretly enjoyed the change from his usually focused and commanding attitude.

"I was just messing around," Artie muttered to her. "You all right?"

"Fine," Lara replied continuing to stare off out the window with an emotionless look.

"Speaking of messing around, since we are almost there, you want to head down to the workout room?" asked Artie pinching at her thigh.

Lara rolled her eyes and hopped off his lap. "Sorry, I've already filled my quota of sparks today."

Artie laughed, knowing his wife wouldn't fall for any more of his cheesy advances. He looked down to see the bracelet on her wrist.

He reached out for her hand and looked down at the hospital tag attached to it. "You ready to take it off this time?"

Lara looked down at her bracelet. "Maybe."

"Un huh. The same way you said you'd take it off the last trip. And the trip before that," said Artie.

Lara pulled her arm away from him. "I'll take it off when I no longer feel like it's our fault."

"It wasn't our fault."

Lara took a deep breath and sighed in frustration. "I'm not arguing about this again. Just let it go."

"I have let it go. Now you need to. I just want to forget about it all and move on," Artie replied.

Lara could feel the anger and frustration rising from her fingertips. "Art! Drop it! Please!"

Artie looked up at her, wishing she would just let go of her guilt already. "Fine. Did Patrick and Lem fix the doors to the storage room?"

Lara stood next to him at the console, wiping the grease and frustration away on her jumpsuit. "I don't know; you'd have to ask them."

Artie swiveled his chair around and leaned forward to the console. He pressed the call button with Patrick's name on it. The console beeped twice as they both waited for a response.

"Yellow?" said a male voice over the speaker.

"You guys fixed that door to the storage room yet," asked Artie leaning toward the console.

"Lem, hand me that box of wire nuts. Uh… No. Was about to when Lem reminded me we still needed to repair the ventilator for the argon tanks," Patrick replied.

"Well once you're done, please fix that. I don't want to be chewed out because the inspection crew can't get in the door. They always look for a reason to cut part of our pay," said Artie.

"Whole damn ship's a floating space dumpster," muttered Patrick over the intercom.

"Yea, well she's my space dumpster, so take loving care of her," said Artie.

"Yea, boss. We'll get it fixed. Lara finished rewiring the defroster on the Schooner?" asked Patrick.

Lara raised her eyebrows at Artie in irritation.

"She's almost done. I'm going down to help her now," Artie replied looking back at her with a smirk.

Lara grinned back at him.

"All right," said Patrick. "How close are we?"

"Seventeen hours away," Artie replied.

"Seventeen hours too many. All right, I'll let you know if we need anything back here," said Patrick.

"Roger that," Artie replied as he hung up the call.

"In seventeen hours, I'll be getting my nails and hair done at the station salon," said Lara leaning back on the console. "Just one massage before we have to head back. That's all I want."

Artie sat back in his chair in thought. "So, about that..."

Lara once more looked over at him with a disapproving scowl, ready to unleash another wave of her wrath down upon her husband. "What?"

"I messaged ahead to the station requesting a week off before we had to take the next shipment."

"What did they say?" asked Lara rising to her feet, Artie having piqued her interest.

Artie looked down and sighed with grief. "They offered us a two-week vacation on the station instead."

Lara stared at him for a moment in astonishment. She laughed with excitement. Artie smiled at her and stood up from his chair as she dove into his arms and kissed him. "So we get two weeks all to ourselves?!" she asked.

"Yup. Just you, me, and the best-imported station food money can buy," Artie replied.

"Paid?" asked Lara.

"Paid."

Lara hugged him once more, feeling utter relief at the news of their much-needed vacation. "Does it come out of our already set vacation time to go see my folks when we get back?"

"Nope. Since we've been with the company for five years now, they are giving us extra time away this year if we requested. When I heard back from them, I wasn't going to argue."

"Ah, I feel so relieved!" said Lara.

"All right. Now let's get to work so we can dock and have our two-week vacation," said Artie. He turned around and set the bridge console to auto before following Lara over to the door to the main deck.

Stepping out into the main deck, Lara stopped at the doorway to the workout room and opened it. She grabbed Artie by the hand and pulled him over toward her.

"Wrong way," said Artie looking at her confused.

"The defroster can wait another hour," Lara replied.

Two

April 30, 2187
- Doris Station -

"Doris Station, this is DATO Six. Do you copy?" said Artie sitting at the console control, speaking into his headset. He tapped his finger on the edge of his chair impatiently, waiting for a reply.

"They're just going to make us wait in orbit," said Lara sitting in the chair next to him.

Artie waited, double-checking that he was indeed transmitting to the station. He could see the shimmer coming off the station's solar panels in the distance. The station orbited the massive asteroid with small tunnels bored out across its jagged black, red, and grey surface.

"Doris Station, this is DATO Six. Do you copy?" Artie repeated into the microphone.

"We've been on our way for twenty-six days. How much more time do they need?" said Lara.

"What's our distance?" asked Artie over to Lara.

"Eight kilometers."

Artie could see the shuttles from the space station making their way to and from the surface of the asteroid, like ants carrying dirt back to their anthill. It was obvious the station was still in full operation, with no excuse for their failure to respond.

"They'd better pick up, or I'm going to dump this cargo out into space," threatened Artie.

"You could, assuming you'd rather have a permanent vacation rather than two weeks," Lara replied.

"DATO Six, this is Doris Station. We copy you. Please confirm your heading," said a voice over the radio.

"Finally," said Artie with relief. "We are eight kilometers out on a heading of fifty-six degrees. Ready for docking confirmation."

"Negative DATO Six. Maintain orbit at a distance of five kilometers with your SOT active and await further confirmation," replied the voice.

Lara laughed and shook her head. "Of course."

"Copy that Doris Station. Adjusting to an orbit of five kilometers and awaiting further instructions," said Artie with an irritated expression.

Artie slapped his hand on the console, ending the transmission. He typed the new trajectory into the computer, then sat back in his chair and glared at the station out the window.

"Never fails," said Lara. "Just like waiting to get off an airplane after a ten-hour flight. They love to make you wait even longer."

The door at the back of the bridge opened. Patrick and Lem walked in and stood on the upper deck balcony looking down at Lara and Artie sitting in front of the window overlooking the ship. Lem removed the clip from the back of her head, letting the long blond and vibrant blue tipped hair on the left side of her head flow freely.

"We get a dock yet?" asked Lem wiping the black smudge under her hazel eye on her left cheek away.

"No. They put us into orbit," said Lara.

Patrick snickered to himself, running his hand back through his crew cut grey and coffee-colored hair. "We've made this run fifty-six times, and every time they put us on hold for another two or three hours. There's always someone who has to ask someone else for docking confirmation, while that person's probably running around asking questions from some other official for two hours. Bunch of monkeys could run the show better."

"Pat, head down to the hangar and load up in the Schooner. Maybe if we are overly prepared they might speed things up," said Artie.

"I'll do it," said Lem with an eager voice.

Artie turned around and looked back at her. "Pat's the only one designated to fly."

"I passed the SS license test yesterday on the computer and Pat's been working with me all week in the hangar. Come on, Cap," pleaded Lem.

Patrick shook his head in agreement. "She's got the right stuff. I wouldn't mind staying on the ship for once."

Artie thought to himself for a moment. He looked over at Lara.

She shrugged at him, letting him know she was going to abstain from the decision. Artie looked back at Lem, who proceeded to clasp her hands together begging to him in silence.

"All right. But keep your mic open the whole time. Pat, take her down and show her everything," said Artie.

Lem smiled with excitement. "Yessss."

Pat grinned at her. "Come on," he said, tugging Lem by the sleeve toward the door.

Waiting for Lem to disconnect the fuel and power lines, Patrick sat in the cockpit running a full scan of the ship's function to make sure everything was in proper working order.

"She good?" asked Lem, stepping into the cockpit door, eager to get her feet wet.

"Yea. Just keep a good distance from the ship and don't turn off the dampeners. Put the space suit on for me too," requested Pat.

Lem glared at him. "I know what I'm doing. I don't need to wear the suit."

"You either put it on, or I'll fly it," threatened Patrick.

Lem grunted and walked to the far wall at the back. She pulled the heavy, thickly-padded space suit out from the closet, and heaved it up onto the hook inside the small spacecraft.

"Everything good down there?" asked Artie from the bridge over the radio.

"Yea, give us a minute. Lem's putting the suit on," Patrick replied.

Artie sat for a moment in confusion. He glanced over at Lara. "Why is he making her put that on?"

Lara laughed. "She's a greenhorn. He's just trying to make things as difficult as possible for her."

Lem finished locking together the top and bottom halves of the suit. She stood up straight, unhooking the suit allowing all the weight to rest on her shoulders. She stumbled for a second, trying to gain her balance. "God, this thing weighs a ton," she said to Patrick.

"Never go out without protection," said Patrick. "It'll weigh less once you get out there."

Lem picked up the suit helmet and held it out to Patrick. "Do I have to wear the helmet too?"

Patrick stood up from the cockpit seat and walked over to her. "No, but keep it close just in case."

"Thank God," Lem replied, stepping past Patrick. She placed the helmet down on the floor next to her and sat down in the cockpit chair and started buckling the harness around her suit.

"Slow and steady. She's not a racecar, so keep the dampeners on and watch your speed. It's like driving a boat and doesn't stop on a dime, so give yourself enough stopping distance," said Patrick stepping out of the cockpit.

"All right."

Patrick reached over and slid the cockpit door closed. He turned the latch with a loud hiss as the remaining pressure in the door escaped.

"We ready?" asked Artie over the speaker.

"Yea," said Lem into the microphone. "Pat's closing me in now."

Lem watched Patrick from the cockpit as he strode his way across the hangar to the elevator door. Waiting for the doors to open, he turned around and gave her a strong salute. Lem reached her arm up to try and return the gesture. The suit and harness held her arms low below the dashboard.

Patrick turned around and stepped into the elevator, watching her through the glass. He tapped on the computer screen of the elevator. "I'm in the elevator. Ready when you guys are."

Artie looked over at Lara and gave her a quick nod. She reached out in front of her and flipped the switch on her control panel. "Rotation disengaged."

They all could feel the subtle spinning motion of the ship begin to come to a halt. Lara watched the ends of her chestnut-colored hair gradually float away from her. She reached into her pocket and pulled out a hair tie to help restrain her now free-flowing locks. Patrick could feel his weight steadily lift away, leaving him clinging to the handle in the elevator.

"Motion's stopped," said Lara into the microphone. "Opening hangar doors."

Lem watched as the large white metallic hangar doors slowly opened, revealing a sea of absolute darkness ahead of her. She flipped the open fuel switches on the control board and placed her finger on the main engine button. She took a moment to herself, hoping her first flight away from the ship wouldn't start with no engines.

Pressing down on the button, she waited impatiently for the sound of the engines firing around the ship. Patrick watched as both rear engines flashed for a moment before firing into an orange glow, which faded to blue. Each of the exterior engines fired one after the other.

Lem smiled, feeling a sense of relief seeing the ship's computer confirming each of the engines had started. "Main engines are hot. Disengaging landing gear."

With a loud thud, the landing gear decoupled from the hangar floor. The ship slowly began to drift around in the hangar.

"Easy does it. Don't burn a hole in the hangar," said Patrick to her over the console.

Lem slowly eased down on the throttle, careful not to run the edges of the ship into the hangar doors. Gently flying out from the hangar, Patrick cringed to himself, watching the top of the ship nearly grind across the top of the hangar door.

With nearly a foot of room left, Patrick let out a sigh of relief in seeing the Schooner float away from the ship free from anymore close calls. "Schooner is away."

Basking in the freedom, Lem watched from the side of her cockpit as the DATO drifted away from her. Coursing her way around the outer edge of the ship, she approached the front of the cockpit, seeing Artie and Lara still sitting at the control panel.

Lara waved at her as she drifted past. "How's the view?"

"Hard to say. Grim, desolate, and lifeless. Outer space looks amazing, though," replied Lem jokingly.

"Hey!" shouted Artie into the mic. Lara and Patrick both laughed. Artie shook his head, "Do a check of the hull while you're out there before I make you bring it back in for insulting my ship."

"Roger that," Lem replied, flying the Schooner toward the back of the ship.

"Here comes the artificial gravity. Make sure you're holding on to something, Pat," said Artie pressing and holding down the artificial gravity button.

Patrick held tight to the handlebar of the elevator. All his weight quickly returned, as the artificial gravity passed down the length of the ship.

"All right, I'm heading to the engine bay if you need me. Keep me posted when we get our docking confirmation," said Patrick.

"Roger that," Artie replied. He sat back in his chair, now left with nothing to do but wait.

Lara could see the worn out look in her husband's eyes, accompanied by the usual stress of docking.

"Go," she said to him.

"What?"

"Go on. Go get some sleep. I'll message you when they call for us."

"I'm fine," Artie replied.

"No, you're not. You're doing that puppy pout of yours that says you're stressing out. Everything's fine. Go, I'll take over," said Lara.

Artie stared out the window. "What about Lem?"

"What about her? She's not going anywhere. She's doing fine out there on her own. She's been with us for two years now. I'd hope you'd have a little more faith in her."

Artie let out a heavy sigh, "All right. Keep me posted if anything happens."

Getting up from his chair, Artie leaned over and kissed his wife on the top of her head.

♦ ♦ ♦

"Art!" shouted Lara over the console speaker in the living quarters.

Artie opened his eyes and stared blankly at the ceiling for a moment. He had just fallen asleep.

Artie jumped up from his bed and walked over to the console in the room. "Yea," he said back to her as he sat up.

"They are ready for us," Lara replied.

"All right. I'm on my way up."

Artie rubbed the sleep away from his eyes as he reached over to the foot of the bed to grab his flight jacket. Slipping an arm into his jacket, he suddenly felt the whole ship change course, gently rolling him back onto the bed.

He stared at the wall for a moment with only one arm in his jacket, his eyes were wide and alert.

The cabin lights went dark. The ships red alert light began flashing followed by the master alarm wailing across the ship's PA.

"ART!" shouted Lara again over the console.

Artie put his other arm in his jacket, trying to hurry over to the console near the door. "What the hell was that?!" he shouted.

"I don't know! Engine four just stopped responding!" shouted Lara over the alarm.

"Shut it down then!" Artie replied.

"I tried already! I can't! Something's wrong!" Lara replied desperately trying to find a way to kill the power to the engine from the bridge.

Artie slammed his hand on the door panel and hurried down the hall at a full sprint toward the elevator. The ship quivered and vibrated under his feet. He could hear the faulty engine trying to power down all the way from the front.

Reaching the elevator, he stepped inside, making his way toward the lower back deck. With little time to waste, he waited impatiently for the elevator doors to open before taking off down the hall.

Opening the engine bay door, he could see Patrick across the bay trying to pry the red manual fuel cutoff valve to the closed position with all his might. The engine room howled with an unsettling sound of the engine sputtering and grinding.

"What's wrong?"

"She won't budge! She's stuck open!"

"Shut it down, Pat!" Artie shouted running over to him.

"I can't! The fuel cutoff is rusted shut and the pressure is too strong!" Patrick shouted back over the grinding sounds from the engine room.

Artie ran over to the communications panel in the engine bay. "Lem! What the hell's going on?!"

Lem flew her way around to the back of the ship as she watched it bank in an unsettling direction. Reaching the back end of the ship, she could see the damaged engine appear all but dark, with only a soft, orange, heated glow from deep within its main chamber.

"I don't know! She's just glowing!" Lem replied.

An unexpected burst of heat erupted from within the engine's core, blasting outward back at Lem in the Schooner. Patrick and Artie both flew to the ground as the tools, and heavy metal crates flew around the room.

Laying on his stomach, he looked up to see a crate barreling its way over toward Patrick. He hastily reached over and grabbed him by the arm, dragged him out of the way of an incoming crate, narrowly saving him from being flattened against the back wall.

The Schooner spun back away from the ship, forced by the ship's unpredicted burst of energy.

"Lem! Lem, you all right?" shouted Lara into her headset.

Lem flailed around in her chair, trying to reach out in front of her and grab the controls as the Schooner tumbled end over end away from the ship, helplessly firing each of its engines in an effort to regain control. The space helmet spun wildly around in the cockpit, smacking her across the forehead.

Desperate to regain control, she finally grasped both controls in her hands, helping guide the ship back under her control.

"Lem!" shouted Lara again.

"Yea! Yea! I'm all right," Lem replied feeling the small gash on her forehead form droplets of blood that drifted around in the cockpit. "Just suffering from a head injury from my helmet is all."

Artie hurried back to his feet and over to the engine bay panel. "Lem! Keep back! If she does that again, I don't want you anywhere near her!"

"Understood!" Lem replied trying to reach up and cover the wound on her forehead.

"Art!" shouted Lara over the alarm. "She just tried to clear her throat and now whatever's in her throat's stopping her from breathing altogether! She's starting to overheat!"

Patrick hurried up from off the floor and ran over to the fuel cutoff valve again. Artie ran back and joined hands with him, trying to pull the long red handle into the off position.

"Come on!" grunted Artie, feeling the muscles in his arms start to tear in desperation.

They both let go and stared at the handle out of breath. "It's hopeless!" Patrick shouted.

Artie looked over at him, then back behind him around the room, hoping to find something to help pry the valve closed.

A fire box hung on the wall, with a hose curled up inside. Artie looked behind him to see the metal belt for the engine's pumps spinning rapidly in perfect sync.

Artie hurried over to the fire box and pulled the hose out.

"Here!" shouted Artie running back over to the lever.

Lem watched from a distance as the ship let out another blast of heat. Artie and Patrick tumbled to the floor once more, desperately grasping at whatever was around them they could hold on to.

"She's at sixty-seven percent! You guys need to shut it down now!" shouted Lara once again over the panel.

Artie and Patrick got back up on their feet. Artie hurried over and handed one end of the hose to Patrick. "Tie this on to the end!"

Patrick looked at him for a moment, confused by his plan. "Now is not a fine time to be watering flowers!"

"Just do it!" Artie shouted back.

Patrick wrapped the end of the hose around the back of the fuel cutoff handle and tied it.

Artie stood in front of the large metal pump belt, with the remaining heavy bundle of hose in his arms.

"Ninety-one percent! Shut it down!" shouted Lara.

"Make a break for the door!" Artie shouted back to Patrick.

Patrick watched, suddenly realizing what his friend and captain was about to do. He hurried over toward the engine bay door.

Artie heaved the end of the hose in one continuous motion into the track of the belt and turned around into a full sprint for the door.

"Run!"

The hose rapidly coiled up into the belt, letting out a loud zipping sound across the bay, until the hose was taught. The end of the lever swiftly slammed over into the off position, before breaking the handle off and bouncing across the room.

The belt came to a grinding halt as the metal ends one by one broke free and began flying around the room in all directions. Artie dove in through the doorway, narrowly avoiding being scalped by a metal shard.

Lem watched as the engine's faint bright heated glow faded.

Artie rolled over and looked back into the doorway as the remaining scraps of metal came to a standstill.

"She's down! "shouted Lara into her microphone with relief. Lara threw her head back into her chair as the alarm finally stopped.

Patrick stood panting with his hands on his knees, offering a hand out to help Artie up off the floor. "You all right?"

DATO

"I'm fine," Artie replied staring into the destroyed engine bay. He gathered a melancholy expression realizing now his two weeks' vacation was probably going to be cut short. Very short.

Three

May 2, 2187
- Doris Station -

Artie opened the door to the conference room to see the three DATO representatives sitting around the cherry wood conference table, each wearing pressed grey business suits, while Artie was dressed in his only white collared shirt and green tie.

"Mr. Glenn, glad you could make it. Have a seat and we'll get things rolling," said the head company representative at the end of the table.

Artie stepped into the room and closed the door behind him. He felt hesitant as he sat down in the vacant conference chair, sensing it was about to be his execution chair.

"I'm Mr. Hidinger, and this is Mrs. Chaffle and Mr. Coppa," said Hidinger introducing the others at the table. "Mr. Coppa, you may start the recording."

Mr. Coppa reached out and tapped on the computer screen embedded into the surface of the table. Artie adjusted his tie nervously and ran his hand back through his hair.

Hidinger cleared his throat and coughed. "The following meetings were conducted on May 2nd, 2187, on Doris Station orbiting asteroid AB265. The following is a meeting called by the Department of Asteroid Terraforming Operations, or DATO, to address the incident involving vessel DATO Six on April 30th, 2187."

Having made his announcement, Hidinger picked up the pages in front of him and began to look them over.

"How long have you been working for us, Mr. Glenn?" asked Hidinger.

"Uh, five years next month," Artie replied.

"You were once a Captain for the American European Unity Military, correct?" asked Hidinger.

"Yes."

"Based on their records, you were on track to do something big. Why the change in profession, if you don't mind my asking?"

Artie felt a sick feeling well up in his throat. "I applied for the military space division, but withdrew my application for... personal reasons."

"I see. Well, before I address why we are here, I do want to thank you for your five years of service with us and your years in the military," said Hidinger.

"Thank you very much, sir," Artie replied.

"On April 30th, you and your crew arrived at Doris Station to deliver your cargo under DATO orders, correct?" asked Hidinger across the table to Artie.

"Yes, sir," Artie replied.

"You were given instructions to change your course and maintain an orbit around the station until you received further instructions. Is this correct?"

"Yes, sir."

Hidinger flipped through his printed records of the ship's communications log with the station. "More specifically, you were directed to orbit with your ship's SOT, otherwise known as Station Orbital Tracker, on and operating while you waited. Is this correct?"

"As much as I can recall," Artie replied.

"Well, according to your ship's records, you turned on your ship's SOT as the order was given. Then, almost ten minutes before to the incident, you turned it off. Do you have any explanation for this?" asked Hidinger staring at Artie rather intently.

Artie stared back, baffled by the latest information. "This is the first time I've heard this news, sir."

"Were you the one who gave the order?"

"No, I left my co-pilot at the console while I rested for a little while until we were given the all clear to dock."

"By co-pilot, you mean your wife, Lara Glenn?" said Hidinger.

"Yes," Artie replied.

"Did she turn off your ship's SOT under your orders?"

"No. She would never do that. She had no reason to, as far as I'm aware," Artie replied, sounding rather irritated by the accusation against his wife.

"Well, the result of turning off your ship's SOT was a failure to track an incoming Skyline communications satellite in orbit around AB265. Without the change in course given from the SOT, your ship's exterior vent for one of the engines met with the satellite, destroying communications with our ground mining teams for several hours, thus costing both Skyline and DATO nearly $250 million in revenue.

"Were it not for your quick actions, and I must admit, a unique solution to your ship's engine overheating, both you, your ship, and crew would have surely perished," said Hidinger.

"Uh, thank you, sir?" replied Artie, not sure if the representative was offering him a compliment.

Mr. Coppa handed Hidinger another paper from his briefcase, then turned to look at Artie with a blank and careless expression.

"Nonetheless, the incident itself was the result of human error, costing the company nearly $61 million in damage to the satellite, and $473 million dollars in repair costs to the destroyed engine."

"What do you mean human error?"

Hidinger set the papers back down in front of him. "Mr. Glenn, unless you can provide the name of the crew member that caused the incident-"

Artie stood up from his seat and leaned forward across the table. "My crew did what they were told! If there is anyone to blame, it is a faulty system, of which I have had issues with in the past."

Hidinger remained calm and tried to wave Artie back down into his seat. "Mr. Glenn, we have conducted our inspection, and the ship's systems have documented no recent faults and a lack of footage of the ship's security during the incident. Which leads us to conclude, it must have been either you or someone else on your crew."

Artie sat back down in his chair.

"Now, as I've said before unless you can provide us with a name-"

"No one on my crew turned it off!"

Hidinger sighed, finding Artie's rude interruptions and inability to cooperate frustrating.

Artie stopped, and took a shallow breath.

"Mr. Glenn, unless you can shed more light on the incident, I'm afraid there is not much we can do. I will admit, I find it hard to believe you would deliberately sabotage your ship, then go through the heroic actions recorded on your ship's logs, just to contradict yourself. However, my employers think otherwise.

"They believe you turned off your ship's SOT to make a claim on the insurance on the incident, and be rewarded compensation. They've also found your lack of a technical officer on a ship designed to be operated by five people unsettling as well. So, it's my word against theirs, with the scale tipped in their favor."

Artie leaned forward and placed his head in the palm of his hands. He was now almost certain he was about to lose both his job and his ship. Five years of uninterrupted service was about to be washed away with dishonor.

"I have convinced them otherwise it seems. Since you did save the ship, as well as your crew, and have a record with the company now with no prior incidents, they are willing to bend the rules. Your contract will not be revoked, and your crew will not be charged with the incident."

Artie felt a major sigh of relief pass over him.

Hidinger smiled at the relief on Artie's face. He glanced back down at the pages in front of him on the table.

"Unfortunately, that sense of relief comes at a price. I see you were recently approved for two weeks paid vacation on Doris Station?" asked Hidinger.

♦ ♦ ♦

Artie opened the sliding door to his temporary home on the station. He walked inside and loosened his tie as he entered.

"You back already? I'm just getting out of the shower. I'll be out in a second," Lara hollered back from the bathroom.

Artie sat down on the teal colored couch and laid his head back. He glanced over at the coffee table to see a printout of the latest news from back home. News had traveled fast. On top of the usual headlines about the atmosphere expansion crisis being debated endlessly or the growth of poverty, he and his crew had already made the bottom left corner.

Financial Fiasco: Whoops!
DATO Crew of Simpletons Cost Millions on Wall Street

Lara stepped out from the bathroom with a towel around her. Her hair still dripping wet. "How'd it go?"

Artie looked back over the couch and threw the paper over into the trash can near the dining table.

Lara looked over at the trash can as she patted her hair dry. "You saw that, huh?"

Artie rubbed his eye, sensing a headache starting to swell. "We didn't lose our jobs or the ship. So, that's something."

Lara let out a sigh of relief. "They say what caused it?"

"Somehow, the SOT was shut off while we were in orbit, and we sucked up a communications satellite," Artie replied.

"They say what caused it?"

"They think someone on the ship turned it off."

"I never got an alert. I never even opened the command for it. I was the only one on the bridge, and I didn't turn it off," Lara replied pleading her case.

"I know, I believe you. I told them that."

Lara moved over to the front of the coffee table. She laid the towel on the back of the couch to dry. "You're doing it again."

Artie looked at her. "What?"

"Your puppy pout. That's not all they told you, was it?" asked Lara.

Artie got up from the couch and walked over to the window. He watched as a square black and silver mining shuttle docked with the station, just in front of his ship receiving repairs in the drydock. A small welding skiff floated around the exterior white and grey surface of his ship, separating the seams of the broken engine so it could be replaced with a new one. He could see the full length of his ship stretch back into the station. Its bone-like design barely fit inside the new drydock, with the oval-shaped bridge at the rear about to scrape along the top overhanging walkway.

Lara stepped up next to Artie and looked out the window. "They're repairing it already?"

"We are going back again," said Artie continuing to look out the window.

"What?! They promised us vacation time!" Lara argued.

"They didn't promise us anything. And even if they did, would you really trust them to keep their promises. You don't get a vacation after you cost a government-funded organization almost a billion dollars in damage. If you have a billion dollars stashed away somewhere, feel free to go down there and hand it to them," Artie replied.

Lara grew infuriated by her husband's accusing tone. "What do you mean *you*? So, you do think I caused all this?"

"I meant we! I know you're not dumb enough to do something that stupid!"

"So, you think I'm dumb!"

Artie shook his head at her, continuing just to watch the ships traverse their way to and from the station. He wasn't going to get into an argument with her when all she was going to do was twist his words. His mother had always told him to keep his mouth shut when conflict arose in marriage, knowing once tensions had been lifted, then was the time to talk.

Lara watched her husband refuse to reply to her, knowing what tactic he had chosen to deflect their argument, one which seemed to work almost flawlessly. "We've been out there for almost five years now. You know how many trips we've made?" argued Lara.

Artie shook his head and walked away from her. He couldn't stay quiet this time. "No, Lara. Please, remind me."

"Fifty-six! We've made fifty-six trips since we started! That's one thousand four hundred and fifty-six days we've been on that ship traveling between stations, and not once have we made a trip down to Earth!" Lara said still standing at the window.

"Guess you can add another thousand on to that," Artie replied sitting back down on the couch.

Lara stood staring at him, a scowling look on her face. "You said seven years. After seven years, we would both get back to the way things were and try again."

"I know what I said," Artie replied staring off into space. "But shit happens."

Lara ground her teeth in anger at her husband. "When do we leave?"

"Two days if the repairs go as planned. Full cargo with extra passengers to make up for the repair costs," Artie replied.

Lara stomped back into the bathroom, and slammed the sliding door with a loud bang.

Artie sat alone on the couch for a moment, wanting to enjoy the silence. But after five years of silence, the busy world around him for once sounded more soothing. He didn't truly believe his wife was the culprit for their misfortune, nor would he have any reason to suspect anyone else on his small crew. The ship's systems had always been known to fail from time to time, which undoubtedly was the case this time, despite what anyone else claimed. Artie had unshakable confidence in his ship and crew, and it wasn't his crew's fault.

Artie got up from the couch and made his way out into the hall. Walking to the apartment door next to his own, he knocked on the door and waited.

The sliding door opened. Patrick stood in his boxers, his apartment dark with blankets over the windows to block out the shifting sunlight outside. His eyes looked tired and puffy.

"How did it go?" asked Patrick squinting at the lights in the hall. He tossed the paper in his hand on the dresser next to him.

"Didn't lose our jobs, but we are going back out again. Vacation's canceled," Artie replied.

Patrick sighed and lowered his head. "Shit. When?"

"Two days or so, depending on how long the repairs take."

"All right. Guess I'll try to enjoy the next two days as best I can then," said Patrick.

"We're taking on another crew member too. Along with full cargo and passengers," said Artie.

"Jesus, that's a full ship."

"The more we take, the quicker we might pay off the debt," Artie replied.

"Yea makes sense," Patrick replied.

"How's Lem?" asked Artie.

Patrick nodded at the door across the hall from him. "Ask her yourself."

Artie turned around and knocked on the door. He could hear rustling around inside of the room of someone trying to get to the door. The door slid open. A woman with red hair stood in the doorway with only a sheet wrapped around her.

Patrick laughed to himself, watching the woman standing in the doorway, unsure how to respond.

"I'm sorry, I must have the wrong room," said Artie confused.

Patrick grabbed his pack of cigarettes from off the end table and put one in his mouth before lighting the end of it, still laughing at the uncomfortable situation he had created.

"Sorry, Cap. I'm here," Lem replied hurrying out from the back of the room over to the door, dressed in only a shirt, a bandage patch hiding under her bangs from her head injury. Lem gave the woman a look of uncertainty.

The other woman turned around and walked back into the room, leaving Lem alone with Artie at the door. "I'll be there in a second," Lem said to her.

Artie raised his eyebrows back at Patrick, then looked back forward at Lem.

"Sorry, Cap. How'd the meeting go?" asked Lem nervously.

"We leave in two days," shouted Patrick across the hall over Artie's shoulder.

Lem looked at Artie in disbelief. "Two days is a lot shorter than two weeks, Cap? Not that I'm sad to hear we didn't lose our jobs, but that's a bummer."

"Yea. We lost our vacation time," Artie replied.

"Both now and when we get to Earth?" asked Lem.

"Yea. You guys are taking on another hand as well," said Artie not wanting a reminder.

"Son of a bitch…" Lem replied. "They don't need to add another person; we can handle-"

"It was my decision. Our ships designed for a five-man crew, and we've been floating by with only four so far."

Lem nodded to him. "He or she?"

"He. And he's only been on three trips on a third-class vessel with not the cleanest track record, so you and Patrick will be in charge of him."

"Fun. Not only do we lose our vacation time, but we get the town fool. No offense, Cap."

"We already took on a town fool two years ago," shouted Patrick.

Lem leaned around Artie and glared at Patrick as he smiled back jokingly.

"How's your head?" asked Artie looking at the bandage.

Lem reached up and rubbed the spot on her forehead. She snickered. "I refuse to tell anyone I received a head injury from a helmet. As far as they all know, it was a flying scrap of metal from when the ship took a hit."

Artie laughed.

"Town fool," Patrick muttered with a grin.

Lem closed her eyes, already feeling exhausted with Patrick's antics. "Now do you guys mind if I get back to…?" Lem nudged her head back at the woman standing in the room.

"Just be back at the dock at eight am on Tuesday so we can load cargo," Artie replied.

"You got it, Cap."

"Here," said Patrick, tossing the remaining pack of cigarettes over to her across the hall past Artie. "You'll want those for later."

Lem looked at the pack for a moment with disgust. She threw them back to him. The pack bounced off his chest and fell to the floor. "I don't smoke trash or cigarettes."

Patrick snickered, as Lem closed the door behind her.

Artie turned around and walked back over to Patrick.

Patrick grinned at him. "If I wasn't a married man, I'd be doing the same thing."

"She can spend her days off the ship however she feels like. Same goes for you since you aren't a married man," said Artie.

"Once you have a son, you'll understand. Marriage isn't just about you and her. Once you have a child together, that marriage becomes unbreakable."

"Could we please change the subject."

"Right, sorry, Boss. Anyway, I don't need all that drama in my life. I sleep. I can hardly sleep a wink while we are on the ship, so now's my chance to make up the last twenty-six days I missed," said Patrick with the cigarette between his lips.

"Speaking of which, thank you for being there when I needed you," said Artie.

Patrick removed the cigarette from his mouth and exhaled. "I should be thanking you. Wasn't for you, I'd be a pancake on the back wall of the engine bay."

"I'm not going to take all the credit," Artie replied.

Patrick grinned at him before placing the cigarette between his lips again. "How's Lara taking it?"

Artie rubbed his forehead, dreading the walk back to his room. "Disappointed would be an understatement I think."

Four

May 4, 2187, 9:00 AM
- Doris Station -

The loud humming of construction cranes pervaded the loading bay. Artie stood at the door, wearing his green captain's jacket, watching the hangar workers load the second cargo into his ship. Each cargo container they loaded was nearly three stories tall on all sides; each filled to the brim with large chunks of mined ore or tanks of gas.

"Captain Glenn?" asked the hangar manager walking over to him, holding a clipboard. His long grey beard swayed as he walked over.

"Yea?" Artie replied.

"Here are the receipts for the second containers," said the manager. He ripped the stack of pink pages out from his clipboard and handed them to Artie. Artie looked at the stack of pages, feeling a familiar sense of being overwhelmed the past two days.

"Gotta say, this is the largest shipment I've ever seen heading out in all my seven years of work," said the manager.

"How much?" asked Artie.

"Three hundred and forty-nine tons. Enough to sink the Titanic," laughed the manager.

Artie flipped through the pink sheets. "I'm used to only getting half this usually."

"At least you guys will have one hell of a payday coming up."

Artie nodded and laughed unconvincingly, knowing he wouldn't see a single penny for his large haul, along with the following fifteen more until he had paid off the damages.

"You sure she can take it?" wondered the manager, looking through the glass of the station to the rigged, white and grey hull of the ship lined up alongside with the airlock.

"She's rated for five hundred thousand. They usually just spread us thin for the next ship coming through, so they have something to ship," Artie replied.

"She's a big ship," said the manager.

"One of the earliest. They started making them smaller after '53 to try and offer more jobs and more frequent shipments since the Cape incident stirred things up."

"That next ship's going to have to wait in that case. This is every container we have available that's ready for shipment. Thanks to you guys, we'll finally get a break around here," laughed the manager walking away.

"You're welcome," muttered Artie under his breath.

Artie looked out across the loading bay to see Lem standing in front of the lengthy line of pallets stacked with food rations for their return journey, taking inventory on her tablet. She glanced up and down through the wrapped boxes, making sure each one was on her list.

Artie wandered over to her, seeing the bandage still on her forehead underneath her blue-tipped blonde and white bangs.

"You're not concussed, right?" he asked her.

Lem laughed, continuing to look through the boxes. "No, Cap. Just dented is all."

"Good. Figured I'd check before we left to find out my crew member didn't account for everything because she was light in the head," said Artie sitting down on one of the boxes. "I wouldn't blame you for requesting medical leave. Abandoning this sinking ship while you still can."

Lem looked up at him. "No, Cap. I wouldn't dream of doing such a thing to you."

She looked over at the ship, watching the workers load the containers. "She's an old and decrepit bird, but she's grown on me in the past two years."

"The feeling's mutual," Artie replied.

"No, two stitches was all I got. A scar for my first time out, and probably my last." She looked back down and continued counting the boxes.

Artie stared at her confused. "Last?"

Lem glanced up at him out of the corner of her eyes. "You're not taking my license away?"

"Why would I? Wasn't your fault," Artie replied with a snicker.

Lem stood up. "I just assumed you-"

"Don't ever assume. Makes an ass out of you and me," Artie replied jokingly.

Lem laughed, feeling embarrassed for entertaining the thought.

Artie reached over across this chest to his jacket sleeve. He grabbed the small fabric patch sewn onto his jacket by the edge and ripped it off. He held it in front of him for a moment, admiring it. He reached across the boxes and handed it to her. "Here's a token for your first flight out."

Lem took the patch from him and looked at it. A lofted angel with open wings was in the center, with the earth floating in the background in space. She looked down at the bottom. The words *Felix Culpa* were embedded in a decorated banner.

"Thanks," said Lem, gazing down at the patch.

"Lara's stepfather gave that to me the day we signed our leasing contract for the ship and officially celebrated that we were going to space. I've had all my luck with it run out it seems. Maybe it'll serve you better then it's served me," Artie replied.

"Felix Culpa. What's that mean?" asked Lem.

"It means 'happy accident.' It's a Latin saying for anything bad that happens in some way has a happy outcome."

Lem laughed, thinking about the patch's meaning.

"Your first time out might have been a catastrophe, but if you hadn't gone out, I wouldn't have had Patrick on the ship where I needed his help," said Artie.

"You saying I couldn't have helped you?" asked Lem, glancing over at him.

Artie shook his head. "Maybe. Not saying you wouldn't have been more help. I'm more comfortable yelling at him though."

"I'll take it as best a compliment as you can muster," Lem replied with a smile. "Thanks, Cap. Means a lot."

"Yea, yea. Enough sapping around. Now get back to work. We got a shitload of stuff to take back with us," he said standing up from the box where he was sitting.

Artie gazed across the hanger, noticing Lara standing at the door to the ship, watching the fourth of many more crates being loaded inside the ship. She looked over at him with a cold stare, then back at the crate being loaded. Artie made his way across the hangar, being careful to avoid the constant moving machinery of the busy hanger.

"You going to speak to me yet?" asked Artie, walking up behind Lara.

"I wasn't planning on it 'til we arrived back at Earth, but if you're going to keep pestering me, then yes," Lara replied.

Lara continued to watch the crates being loaded with her back to him. Artie stepped around to her side. She had locked him out of their bedroom for the past two days, forcing him to sleep on the more comfortable station apartment couch, and only now was he starting to notice the bags under her eyes.

"You okay?" he asked her.

"No, I have a husband who inside thinks I'm both dumb and accident-prone. Otherwise, I don't know what you mean?" asked Lara not bothering to look over at him.

"Have you been sleeping on that bed in the apartment, or just depriving me of it?"

Lara didn't respond. She stared at him out of the corner of her restless eyes, before wandering away toward the hangar office. Artie followed her.

"What else am I supposed to say, Lara? I've told you I'm sorry every night the past two days. Believe me, if there was another word that could of had any deeper meaning, I'd use it to express my apology," said Artie trailing behind her.

"There is. You just haven't said it," Lara replied opening the door to the office and stepping inside.

Artie stood at the door, thinking carefully about what he hadn't yet said to her. "What is it?" he asked her.

"Jesus, Art. I'll give you a hint; it's three words. Probably the oldest three words in human history," said Lara turning back to him.

"I'm *very* sorry?" Artie replied questioning.

Lara rolled her eyes at his response. "You told me every form of apology you can think of, but I'm not looking for an apology. I'm looking for your comfort. Ever since we started this *stupid* dream of yours, I honestly followed you in the hopes a few years in space would help break that stone shell of yours."

Artie put his hands out in admittance. "What? What am I supposed to say?!"

"I love you God damn it!" Lara shouted.

A few of the dock workers looked back over at the two of them in the office, having obviously heard Lara's shouts from inside. Artie pretended like nothing was happening. He stood in the doorway, petrified by his inability to say the three words that meant everything to any loving couple. He lowered his hands in surrender. "I'm sorry…"

Lara glared over at him.

"I mean… I love you… God damn it!"

Lara's aura of tension subtly softened by his words. She stared down at the computer with all the cargo listed on it, trying to keep her rock-hard composure.

"I know I've not been the best in this relationship since we started this whole thing," said Artie stepping over toward her.

"You weren't very good at it before then, either. Night after night coming home late from the base, leaving me to go to family events alone."

"I was trying to start something for us."

"And then we started something together. And just when I thought you would finally start spending more time with me and playing your role, God punished us both for no reason."

Artie glanced down at the bracelet on her wrist, reading the name on the plastic hospital tag.

Caitlyn Emilia Glenn
DOB: May 4, 2183
6.2 lbs   Dr. C. Becker

"Tomorrow's her birthday," said Artie.

Lara wiped the water away from her eyes, staring at the computer screen. "Why do you think I can't sleep?"

Artie reached out and grabbed Lara by the arm and pulled her over toward him.

She stood in front of him, sniffing.

"Look at me," said Artie to her.

Lara looked up at him, brushing the tear from her cheek.

"You and I may never know why, but what we've been through has made us a couple capable of getting through anything. Life has already beaten us down for us to get back up again, and now we know there's nothing worse that could happen. Once we are finished, I promise that'll be the end of it."

Lara laid her head on his chest, as he wrapped his arms around her. She felt like she could just fall blissfully asleep in his arms.

"We have to let go and move on. Our love for her isn't going anywhere. She's still with us, no matter where we go," said Artie into her ear.

Artie stepped back and reached down to grab Lara's hands. He held her wrist with the bracelet on it out in front of her. "There's no better time to start moving forward."

Lara took a deep sigh and stared down at the bracelet. Every power in her being didn't want to let go, but she knew he was right. She had been holding on for long enough but didn't believe she had the courage to move on.

Artie released her, leaving her to make her decision.

Slipping the bracelet from her wrist, Lara held it in her hand and stared down at it. She clutched her hand around it tightly. She stepped over to the trashcan in the office and stood in front of it for a moment.

Artie watched her, hoping she would let go, ready to move on and quit holding on to the past.

Lara kneeled down and held her hand out over the trashcan. She could see the face of her newborn child, robbed of her life just as it had begun. The last piece of her was resting in her hands.

She sniffed and opened her palm, letting the bracelet fall with a heavy weight.

She stood back up and stared down at the trashcan.

Artie felt a wave of relief pass over him.

Lara looked over at him, the sorrow still heavy in her gaze. She walked back over to him and buried her face into his jacket. Artie kissed her on the head and rested his cheek on her.

"Boss," said Patrick stepping into the office. He stopped and stared at them for a moment silently waiting until they were finished. Artie continued to make him wait, knowing this moment couldn't need his full attention. His wife needed him.

Lara lifted her head away from him and turned away from Patrick while she recomposed herself. Artie turned around to Patrick.

"Our other cargo is waiting over at hangar three for us. One of them wanted to talk to you about some special items he needs to be loaded," said Patrick.

"Yea, we'll head over there right now," Artie replied.

Patrick nodded to him and looked at Lara for a moment. Lara wiped her nose and turned around to look at Patrick, her eyes red and her cheeks spotted. Patrick walked away, trying to give them their space.

Artie turned toward Lara. "I'm going to head to hangar three. You want to meet me over there when you're ready?"

"Yea," Lara replied.

Artie kissed her on the forehead and hurried away out the door. Lara looked over at the trashcan, still feeling the same sense of guilt and sorrow.

♦ ♦ ♦

Patrick stood waiting at the door to hangar three, having no urge to step inside. Artie hurried his way down the stairs at the end of the hall and turned the corner to see Patrick biting his thumbnail as he waited.

"Where is he?" asked Artie.

Patrick pointed inside with the hand that was up to his mouth.

Artie walked over and looked inside the hangar. The dock worker was arguing with a man dressed in a pressed, grey, company suit, with finely combed grey hair and a thick beard. Behind the man were his two associates; a woman with long black hair, and a young man with glasses, tan skin, and wavy brown hair. The man shouted at the worker, while the other workers all stood by and watched the drama play out on the sidelines.

"I'd be extremely careful putting my hand into that lion's den," said Patrick over to Artie.

Artie stepped inside, approaching the two men arguing, ready to defuse the situation.

"They do not stack! I specifically requested this on my forms!" shouted the man in his sharp Italian accent.

"And I'm trying to tell you, if we don't stack them, we'll never fit all of them! If you just left half of them here, we would gladly put them on the next ship!" shouted the dock worker back to the other man gesturing to all the crates around them.

"That's unacceptable! My team and I require the full twenty-six days with each of our collected samples!"

Artie put his hands out ahead of him, ready to arrange a peace treaty between the two men. "Excuse me. What seems to be the problem here?"

"I have no time for this," said the dock worker turning his back on the argument.

"And who might I ask are you to be taking charge over this Neanderthal?" asked the man in a rather unmannerly tone.

Artie turned toward him, with one eyebrow raised. "I'm Captain Artie Glenn. I'm the owner of this ship."

The man gave a brief sigh of relief. "I do apologize for my rudeness in that case. I'm Dr. Pino Pindrazi, project director for AB265 through 278," replied Pindrazi extending a handshake.

"Pleasure," said Artie shaking his hand, feeling less than pleasured.

"And these are my assistants, Annie Tolf, and Rupert Larkvia," said Pindrazi stepping aside. The two assistants placed their shoulder bags down on the floor and stepped forward and shook Artie's hand.

Artie looked around the hanger, admiring the rather large collection of crates the doctor had assembled. "I see you travel light?"

"Indeed. As we've conducted our mining operations on the surface of AB265, we've gathered a rather vast collection of interesting subjects. Many of which we hoped to study on our long voyage back to Earth. So, we will require a rather large area to conduct our research, rather than this broom cupboard we are currently arranged in," said Pindrazi.

"I see," Artie replied. He glanced over to see the dock worker roll his eyes. "Well, if the starboard storage isn't large enough, I could always move you to one of the ship's rear cargos. It's close to the engine room and is noisy at times, but it's currently vacant and rather spacious. We only use it for backup storage in case we have a breach in one of the other holds."

"That would be much appreciated, Captain. The more space we have to work with, the better," replied Pindrazi.

Lara opened the door to the hangar and walked inside, her hands in her pockets, with the same sorrowful expression on her face. A forklift carrying a large crate low to the ground suddenly screeched to a halt, narrowly stopping before it ran into her. The metal crate slammed against the back of the forklift, with a loud bang.

A low, animal-like groan came from inside the crate. Lara looked over at it, hearing the ominous sound. Through the small narrow slits in the crate, the shimmer of four silver eyes caught her attention and stared back at her. All four eyes blinked in unison.

"Hey!" shouted Pindrazi at the forklift driver as he ran over and pointed a finger at him. "That crate is not to be moved unless I say so! Understood?!"

The forklift driver nodded to him, with an innocent look on his face. Pindrazi stepped back from the forklift watching the driver intently as he drove away with the crate. Lara continued to stare at the crate, unsure what she just saw.

Artie hurried over to Lara. "Uh, Dr. Pindrazi, I would like you to meet my wife, Lara."

Pindrazi extended a hand out to her.

Lara looked away from the crate and over at the doctor standing in front of her. She reached out and shook his hand. "Uh- I'm sorry. I just was lost in thought for a moment. A pleasure to meet you."

"Yes. Well, not that I don't enjoy meeting you both, but I'm not one for awkward social interactions. I don't expect us to all become acquainted during our voyage, except during perhaps meals and other rare occasions," said Pindrazi.

"Of course," Artie replied, unsure of how to respond. "I'll inform the dock manager of the change, and we'll have the ship moved into place to have your cargo moved on in the next hour or so hopefully."

"Much appreciated, Captain. Ma'am," said Pindrazi to Lara before turning around and walking back over to his assistants.

Artie and Lara watched him walk away with his arms crossed behind his back. They both turned around and walked back over to the hangar door where Patrick continued to stand with his elbows resting on the safety railing.

"Temperamental little cuss, ain't he?" said Patrick as Artie and Lara walked over.

Artie looked back at Pindrazi as he talked to his assistants. "Personality like a coin. He's heads one minute, then tails the next."

"Let's all just pray that he keeps to himself like he says," said Patrick standing up.

"Come on," said Artie turning his attention back to Patrick. "We still have a lot of work to get done before we are ready to leave."

"Don't remind me," Patrick replied, turning around and walking back out the hangar door.

Artie began to follow him. He glanced back to see Lara still staring over at the crate being put away. "Hey?" Artie stepped back and placed a hand on her shoulder.

Lara turned around and looked at him. "What?"

"You all right?" asked Artie.

"Fine. Just tired I guess," Lara replied.

"Well, let's try and finish up what needs to be done. Then you can sleep for twenty-six days while I fly us back home."

"Yea," Lara replied seeming distant.

Artie turned around and walked out the door. Lara followed him, glancing back briefly at the crate once more.

Five

May 4, 2187, 5:50 PM
- Doris Station -

    Artie waited at the entrance to the gangway of the ship with Lem and Lara at his side. The elevator at the end of the corridor opened to the sounds of a large group starting to make their way down the hall toward them.

    "That sounds like them," said Lara leaning forward to see around the corner.

    The group of nine passengers turned the corner carrying their luggage, each dressed in their blue flight suits, some with their appointed military patches.

    "You guys DATO Six?" asked one of the young men with a sharp crew cut at the front of the group.

    "Yes, sir," replied Artie.

    The young man threw his navy-blue duffle bag down on the ground and saluted. "You must be Captain Glenn. Pleasure to meet you, sir."

The other three military members of the group dropped their bags and saluted.

"At ease. You all can relax. I've been out of the service for five years now, and I won't hold you to any military standards onboard. As far as I'm concerned, you all deserve some time to yourselves."

Lara glared over at Artie. If there was anyone onboard the ship that 'deserved some time' to themselves, it was her and the rest of the crew in her mind.

The young man lowered his hand. "Glad to hear it, sir. Sergeant Cernan at your service, sir. This is Corporal Krantz. Behind me is Private Schmitt, and Private Young, and our fellow mining team members, Collins, Stafford, Lovell, Shera, and White."

"This is my first mate, Lara, and my second engineering officer, Lem," Artie replied.

One by one the group shook hands with Artie, Lara, and Lem.

"Should be a pretty straightforward flight for everyone. Twenty-six days to Earth, non-stop. We have cabins for each of you on the living deck, so feel free to try and make yourselves at home as best you can in our bathroom-sized bedrooms. Lara will go ahead and show you all around, and we'll leave here in the next hour or so. So, go ahead and get yourselves comfortable," said Artie to everyone.

"Roger that, sir," replied Cernan, offering another salute.

Artie sniggered and shook his head at him. Cernan smiled back and picked his bag up off the ground.

"All right, everybody, please follow me," said Lara opening the door to the gangway. The large group of passengers all began filing into the doorway, with Artie and Lem standing by as they continued to wait.

"Nine mining passengers, plus three station employees, that's all twelve passengers. Now we are just waiting on one more," said Artie, looking around.

"He ever show up for loading?" asked Lem.

"No, and he had better hurry it up if he wants to stay on my good side."

"You didn't meet him before you hired him?"

Artie glanced over at her. "Out here in some of the deepest parts of space, your options become rather limited. It was either him or an older woman who was as old as the space program."

Lem squinted with repugnance. Imagining if she was the captain of her own ship, she'd probably make the same choice.

Artie looked over at Lem's shoulder. She had already sewn the patch he gave her onto the sleeve of her jacket.

Lem noticed him looking at the patch. "Hasn't brought me any luck yet, but I'm still keeping my eyes open."

Artie grinned at her. He leaned forward to see down the hall, growing impatient with his new crew member. "Rub it for me. Maybe this guy will hurry it up."

Lem reached across her chest and started rubbing the patch vigorously with her fingertips. The doors to the elevator soon opened. A young man with dark colored skin and curly black hair walked out with his head phones on, wearing his tattered flight suit with a bag over his shoulder. He quietly muttered the words to the music he was listening to as he shuffled his way over toward them.

"Guess it worked," said Lem.

The young man walked up to the two of them, still rubbing the sleep from his eyes. He removed a headphone from his right ear. "You Captain…" The young man reached into his bag and pulled out a crumpled up blue slip of paper and unfolded it, "Glenn?"

"Maybe. You Cliff?" asked Artie.

"Maybe. Assuming you can give me a good reason to work on your ship."

Artie looked at him confused. "Because you've been instructed to?"

"Yea, but as an employee, I reserve the right to refuse service on any ship I don't deem worthy of my skills."

Lem smirked, watching Artie's attitude fade into his commanding military background. She knew this new crew member was about to see her captain's real colors.

"And as a captain, I have a right to leave your ass behind and write you up as unreliable, forcing you to wait for the next civilian transport in five months to take you home without any payment. Then I'd leave without a second thought."

"I don't appreciate the attitude, even from a Captain. But fine, I guess you've made a solid point," replied Cliff crumpling up the paper and putting it back in his pocket.

"You never came to load this morning," Artie replied.

"Overslept. No one told me I needed to help load anyway. I'm the guy with the brains, not the brawn."

Artie stared at him. He obviously wasn't the strongest person, and he hadn't shown any signs of intelligence, making Artie question his true worth. He could already sense he and his new technical engineer were going to bump heads the whole trip.

"Lem," said Artie all of a sudden. "Meet your new crew member. Cliff, meet Lem. She's your second engineering officer."

"Nice to meet you," Cliff replied observing Lem from top to bottom.

Lem let out a disgusted grunt, already knowing what was going through his conceivably perverted mind.

"Lem, why don't you go ahead and show Cliff around the ship and where he will be staying," said Artie continuing to stare at Cliff, still trying to judge whether to leave him or let him on board.

"What?! You're going to leave him with me?"

Artie turned around and stepped into the gangway. "We leave in an hour!"

Lem stood in the doorway, in utter disbelief. She looked back over at Cliff. Cliff smiled at her and stood idly with his hands behind his back listening to his music.

Lem grunted once more and turned around, "Come on before I leave you here."

♦   ♦   ♦

Stopping in front of the cabin door, Lem waited for Cliff to catch up while he looked down to his music player. At the other end of the living quarters, Lem could hear the group of passengers getting their tour of the ship from Lara.

"Hey! You want to hurry it up!?" yelled Lem back at him.

Cliff looked up at her, and back down at his music player as he continued to walk at his own pace.

Lem walked over to the living quarter's hallway and opened the vacant crew cabin door. Lem stepped inside and waited while Cliff stood in the doorway. Cliff's eyes glanced up away from his music player to see the small enclosed living space, no bigger than a small bathroom.

"Nice closet," he said to her.

"It's your room," Lem replied.

Cliff stared at her confused. "Seriously?" He stepped inside and began scanning the room, already starting to feel claustrophobic. "This ship is as big as a skyscraper! You've got to be joking me!"

"Nope, only one that is bigger than this is the Captain's quarters, and it's only a few feet wider with a bigger bed. Ship's meant to be a carrier, not a luxury cruise."

Cliff threw his bag down on the small single sized bed. He moved around behind Lem and slid open the door to the bathroom and stuck his head through the door. The shower was only a few feet wide, with only a foot of space between the toilet and sink. Cliff pulled his head back through the door and slid it closed with a sigh of disbelief. "Last time I travel coach," he said to himself.

Lem pulled open the closet doors next to her. "Closet's not much bigger, but it's roomier than the bathroom," she said.

Cliff glanced over at her, noticing her back was turned. He stepped up close behind her, brushing up against her with his waist. Lem stared ahead of her and gritted her teeth, knowing what he was trying to do.

"Cozy enough for two people I'd say," said Cliff sniffing her hair.

Lem reached up above her and pulled down on the overhead closet door. She leaned her head to the side out of the way as the door swung down and smacked Cliff on the top of the head behind her.

Cliff grumbled and stepped back away from her, rubbing the top of his head.

"Whoops. Sorry about that," she said to him in a sarcastic tone. "Should have warned you about the overhead doors. You can put your shoes or anything you don't need in the overhead closet."

Lem made her way back out into the hall, with Cliff still standing in the room, feeling the lump starting to form on the top of his head.

"Laundry is down that hall. Don't use it if we aren't rotating or the artificial gravity isn't on, obviously. Come on. I still need to show you the rest," she said to him.

Cliff followed her out into the hall, and over to the elevator. Stepping into the elevator, Lem tapped on the panel with Cliff standing next to her.

"If you need to get around the ship, use the elevator. There are three decks, each connected by the elevator, bow, stern, port, starboard, all of it," said Lem watching the elevator doors close. "Top floor is life support systems, recycle tank storage, and a few small storage areas. Second level and midship are mostly living quarters, the infirmary, a small atrium, and water recycling. And the third deck is all cargo, with the loading bay where we keep our dinghy ship for docking. The back of all three is the bridge, power, and engine bay."

"You know, you don't have to be shy around me," said Cliff.

Lem looked over at him. "All right, I'm just going to let you down now before you start getting any ideas and I'm stuck with you the rest of the trip; One, you're annoying. Two, you're not even my type. And three, I pitch for the other team. So, if you don't want to wake up with anything missing one morning, you keep your distance from me. Understood?"

Cliff stared at her blankly, followed by his smug smile. "No problem, baby."

Lem snarled and turned back around away from him. Cliff and Lem both stood quietly for a moment, waiting for the elevator to stop and move to the next floor in a horizontal fashion.

"So, what's Captain Attitude's problem?"

"Other than you, now, a lot of things," said Lem.

"Such as?" asked Cliff.

Lem looked over her shoulder back at Cliff. "He owes the company an assload of money now, and lost his only vacation time in five years."

"So, it was you guys who crashed into that com satellite and caused the blackout," said Cliff laughing. "I heard the news already made it across the system. You guys are now the new face of screw-ups everywhere."

"Yea, and you're now the newest honorary screw-up."

The elevator doors opened just in time for Lem to get away from her new admirer. She stepped out into the dark corridor of the ship and flipped on the lights.

She pointed over to the door next to her. "Your office is in there."

Cliff pulled his headphones out from his ears and opened the sliding doors. Inside was a long array of shelves, each one part of the ship's central server. Cliff stepped inside and began wandering through the rows one by one. "This computer is twenty years old. Shit, even older than that. Older than me by the looks of it," said Cliff.

"You'll have plenty of time to work on improving it then," said Patrick stepping into the doorway next to Lem.

"Patrick, Cliff. Cliff, this is Patrick, your boss and mine down here," said Lem.

Cliff stood up and snickered, looking over at Patrick. "Ship's a museum, both inside and out."

Patrick raised his eyebrows and glanced over at Lem. "Spice under the collar," said Patrick. "I'm sure Artie's already sold on you."

Lem nodded toward Patrick, "He's the reason the gene pool needs a lifeguard in my opinion."

Cliff blew the dust off the central server panel cover and unfastened the clamps. A small cloud of dust billowed out and into his face. "You guys ever bother to clean this thing?" said Cliff coughing.

"That's what we have you for now," said Patrick. "We've been cleared to leave whenever."

"All right. I'll meet you in back once I've done my rounds," said Lem.

Patrick nodded and turned toward Cliff. "Welcome aboard, kid. Hope you enjoy your twenty-six days."

"Thanks," said Cliff unenthusiastically, continuing to wipe the dust away from the shelf with his palm.

Patrick turned around and walked out of the room, leaving Lem and Cliff alone once more.

"You need anything, keep it to yourself. Unless it's so important you have to bother someone," said Lem. "And don't do anything stupid please."

Cliff glanced over at her and smiled, still kneeling at the base of the central server. "Anything for you, sweetheart," he replied.

Lem grunted in disgust. She turned around and walked out of the room, leaving Cliff alone with the ship's computer.

"It's going to be a long twenty-six days," said Cliff pulling out another dusty component with a look of disgust on his face.

♦ ♦ ♦

Artie stepped onto the bridge with a dispirited expression. Lara sat in her chair at the console, seeing Artie shake his head in disappointment at her.

"What?" she asked him.

Artie sat down in his chair and looked over at her.

"What? What is it?" She was growing frustrated by her husband's lack of a response.

"The new guy," he replied.

"What about him?"

"Kid's already skating on thin ice. Shows up late and starts off on the wrong foot right out the gate," said Artie.

"Just keep your distance from him. I'm sure Pat and Lem can handle him," Lara replied, opening the ship's controls on her screen. "Now let's get out of here before I decide to leave you for a younger pilot on this station."

"Ready when you are."

Lara reached ahead of her and tapped the open intercom button on her screen. The speakers across the ship groaned and whistled with feedback. "Attention passengers and crew members, this is first officer, Lara Glenn, from the bridge. Please locate a flight seat near you and prepare for departure in the next five minutes."

Lara tapped on the screen once more, ending her announcement to everyone.

"All right," said Artie grabbing the flight controls on both sides of his chair. "Let's take this slow and steady. I don't want to demand too much of that new engine."

Lara tapped on the glass computer screen in front of her, pulling up the diagram of the ship. Pressing the red disengage command on the screen, they could hear the station's grasp on the ship clatter as each clamp released. The ship trembled under them.

"We're free," said Lara watching the screen.

The massive ship slowly began to drift away from the station, with each gentle burst from the ship's starboard engines pushing them laterally. Twisting the controls in the palm of his hands, Artie started to rotate the ship away from the station.

"Now if she lights, we'll be in business," said Lara.

Artie reached out ahead of him and tapped the engine ignition button at the center of the console. They both waited eagerly, awaiting the rattle of the ship to signify the engines had all ignited.

The ship continued to drift away from the station, still waiting for the engines to fire.

"Well this is off to a great start," said Artie glancing over his control panel to make sure he didn't miss anything.

"Patrick!" Shouted Lara into the microphone on her console.

"I got it. I got it," Patrick replied into his radio. "Some jackass never turned the new fuel valve on."

"I hope you're not talking about yourself," said Artie into his microphone.

Patrick huffed into the microphone, followed by a brief grunt as he rolled the valve open. The sound of the argon gas and liquid fuel rumbling through the pipes in the engine bay.

"All right, should be on now," replied Patrick.

"Let's try this again," said Artie.

Tapping the ignition button once more, the ship immediately shook as the engines each fired all0 together in sync. Lara and Artie both let out a sigh of relief.

"Now can we go?" asked Lara, growing eager.

Artie tapped the microphone intercom button. "Flight crew and passengers, prepare for takeoff in t-minus thirty seconds." The clock on his dashboard started the count. He reached down to his side and grabbed his harness belts and began fastening them tightly across his chest.

"Ten seconds," he said looking up at the clock. "Nine. Eight. Seven. Six."

Lara pressed her head back against her seat in preparation. "Five. Four. Three. Two. One."

Artie tugged on the throttle handle at his right side until it was all the way back. The ship rumbled under their feet as they gradually began to pick up speed. Artie followed the trajectory line projected on the glass windshield ahead of him, steering them on a course back toward Earth.

Watching the thrust gauge roll over, the two of them could feel their shoulders sink into their seats.

"Forty thousand meters," said Lara reading the numbers on her dashboard. "Seventeen thousand."

Artie watched as the numbers on the screen began to settle at eighteen thousand. "Flight crews prepare for second stage," said Artie.

Artie reached out ahead of him and flipped open the safety cover over the illuminated, blue, second stage ignition button. He pressed it firmly for one second and held on to the controls.

A loud boom roared throughout the ship, accompanied by a sudden jolt. They could feel the ship around them beginning to hurtle off into space with their heads firmly pressed against the back of their seats. The numbers on the dashboard flashed across the screen.

"Twenty thousand. Thirty. Forty. Fifty," said Lara over to Artie. "Approaching target velocity."

The numbers on the screen all started easing to a stop. "Eighty-seven thousand," said Lara. The weight which forced them back into their seats gradually lifted away, allowing them to move finally. Artie rolled his head around across his shoulders.

"Initiate roll," said Artie over to her.

Lara tapped on her screen. They both watched the stars out the window ahead of them subtly begin to rotate toward their heading.

"And.... we are at one G," she said to him. "All right. We are on our way."

"Attention all crew and passengers. We have reached our target velocity, and you are now free to move about the ship at your leisure. Our arrival at Earth is now estimated at Twenty-five days, twenty-three hours, and forty-nine minutes in counting. Bridge signing off," said Artie into his microphone.

"You're normally not so formal about that," said Lara.

"Something tells me this won't be the last time we have to take passengers with us," Artie replied unbuckling his seatbelt.

Six

May 8th, 2187
- 22 Days Left -

The elevator door to the lower deck opened. Artie stepped out and walked down the hall to see Lem and Patrick both watching the television screen in the kitchen, still finishing their breakfast.

"Morning," said Artie, as he opened the cupboard door and pulled out an airtight bag of cereal.

"Morning, Cap," said Lem, taking another bite of her toast.

"Morning, Boss," said Patrick, with his eyes still glued to the television screen.

Artie peeled open his bag of food and poured it out into a plastic bowl from the cupboard next to him.

"Can you believe this shit?" said Patrick shaking his head at the television.

"What?" asked Artie turning around.

"The CEO of Skyliner Engineering has gone missing. Just straight-up vanished," Patrick replied. "Guy's worth at least forty-six billion dollars, and no one knows where he went."

Artie watched the television screen. A news reporter standing outside a large, tan-colored mansion was talking about the story.

"You mean the same Skyliner Engineering that made the ship?" asked Artie.

"And every other private company invested in space travel? Yea," said Patrick.

"Probably ran off with some girl," said Lem watching the screen.

"That, and the case against the Orlinia mayor just randomly came up with the pictures they needed to put him away. Just right out of the blue, no explanation," said Patrick.

"Probably staged them," Artie muttered.

"No, they analyzed them. It's him all right, and that woman he was working with trying to cover it all up. Supposedly, she works for Skyliner as well."

"Weird," Artie replied.

Artie glanced around the room as he ate his breakfast, noticing his newest crew member had once again not shown his face for the fourth morning in a row.

"You guys see the new guy this morning? I asked him to get to work on upgrading the main computer today."

Patrick and Lem both shrugged. Neither one of them had seen him.

Artie grunted and placed his bowl down on the counter. He walked out into the hall and opened the door to the living quarters. To no surprise, Cliff's door was closed. Artie opened the door to the sight of Cliff draped over his bedside asleep in his boxers, headphones still in his ears with his mouth hanging open, oblivious to Artie's presence in the room.

"Cliff," said Artie calmly, standing at his bedside.

Cliff closed his mouth and swallowed with his eyes still closed. He rolled over on his side and continued to sleep.

"Cliff!" shouted Artie gradually starting to grow impatient.

Cliff remained undisturbed.

Artie forcefully drove his foot into the edge of his mattress, shaking the bed. "Cliff!"

Cliff rolled over again on his side and draped his bed sheet back over him, adjusting the headphone in his ear with his free hand.

Artie ground his teeth. He turned around and walked back over to the control panel in the room, and tapped on the screen to use the intercom. "All passengers, be advised, we will be experiencing some slight turbulence."

Artie typed his password into the panel, and accessed the main deck controls, turning off the rotation of the ship with one quick tap on the screen. The inertia of the rotating cargo ship gradually came to a halt. Artie reached over and held onto the edge of the closet, waiting patiently.

Rising slowly from his bed, the startling sensation of freefall woke Cliff from his sleep into sheer panic. Flailing helplessly over his bed, he became entangled in his sheets.

Artie reached back over to the panel and repressed the same button again. The false sense of gravity returned to the ship. Cliff bounced off the back wall next to his bed and tumbled to the floor. He sat up and stared at Artie in anger.

"Morning," said Artie.

"What the hell?!" shouted Cliff back at him.

"Get up. Time to get to work. The computer isn't going to update itself."

Cliff stood up promptly and walked over to the control panel next to Artie. He tapped on the screen, pulling up the ship's central server. Cliff stepped aside and pointed at the screen with a furious look.

Artie looked over and gazed at the screen. The ship's computer was operating at one hundred and five percent, a reading he hadn't seen since the day the ship was first launched. He looked back over at Cliff, now staring at him with a scowl. His bottom lip curling forward in the same manner as his brow.

"I work while everyone is sleeping," said Cliff.

Cliff turned around and grabbed his bedsheet from off the floor, and laid back down on his bed. Artie stood idly next to the door, unsure of what to say.

"You have an hour, then go help Lem with whatever job she is working on," said Artie, walking back out the door.

Cliff slipped his headphones back into his ears and tossed in his bed trying to get comfortable again.

Stepping out into the hall once more, Artie stood next to the door for a minute. The cabin door just down the hall opened. Cernan stuck his head out, dressed in a wet towel, dripping wet with soap, coughing.

"Trouble with the shower, Sergeant?"

"What's wrong? Everything All right?" asked Cernan.

"Fine. Just had a little malfunction with the rotation," Artie replied.

Cernan nodded and pulled his head back in to his room with a sense of relief. Artie snickered to himself. He turned around and walked back out into the main hall and walked into the kitchen. Lem stood at the kitchen sink trying to clean the spilled orange juice her shirt with a wet towel.

"What was that all about?" asked Patrick. "I don't recall any malfunctions."

"Just keeping everyone on their toes," Artie answered. He looked down at the floor to see his breakfast now spilled out across the cupboards and floor. He sighed, now becoming another victim of his shenanigans.

♦ ♦ ♦

Exiting the elevator, Lara reached up and rubbed the sleep away from her eyes while holding onto the tray she was carrying. Down the wide, grey, metallic hallway of the second floor, she stopped at the door to the cargo bay, now turned into a makeshift laboratory being used by Pindrazi and his assistants.

Peeking through the glass window, she could see the doctor lecturing his assistants, waving his hands wildly in frustration. Both assistants stared blankly at him, unsure how to respond to his odious outburst. Lara opened the door, hoping her very presence would save his young pupils from any more humiliation.

"You replace another sample without cleaning your workstation again, and I will make damn well sure you don't ever receive your doctorate. Understood?!" shouted Pindrazi.

"Morning, everyone," said Lara loudly over him.

The doctor cleared his throat and turned around, transforming himself into his not so convincing opposite person. "Good morning, Mrs. Glenn."

"I brought you all down a few breakfast items from our kitchen if you all are hungry?" said Lara placing the tray down on the computer desk.

Both the assistants looked at the doctor with uncertainty. He looked back at both of them trying to let go of the incident. "Go on," he said calmly.

Both lab assistants hurried over to her, grabbed a muffin and bottled drink and thanked her. Rupert and Annie sat down at their workstations, gorging into their meals. Pindrazi walked over to the tray and picked up the last remaining muffin. "I've never been a fan of banana nut, but I suppose something to eat is better than nothing at all."

"We have more options up in the kitchen. I could bring you back something else," offered Lara.

"No, no. I will live, but thank you for the offer," he replied.

Lara looked around the room, as he sniffed the muffin with disgust and took a bite. Despite the amount of space in the cargo hold, the doctor and his assistants seemed to keep their workstations close to one another, with each of their cargo containers lining the surrounding walls.

Without fail, Lara's eyes became fixed on the strange container she saw from the loading dock, resting in the shadows just out of sight.

"What is it you are working on down here if you don't mind my asking?" queried Lara.

The doctor swallowed his small nibble from his muffin and stared up at her. He noticed her staring across the room at the container, and subtly stepped in the way of her wandering gaze.

"Projects that help benefit humankind, naturally. Many of my fellow researchers back home fail to realize what secrets can be uncovered while collecting resources from our systems' asteroids. Some studies have even proven new developments in areas we never believed possible."

"Like what?" wondered Lara.

Pindrazi stared at her, seeing her eyes trying to peer through him at his work. "It wouldn't be much of a secret if I told you, of course. Though I'm sure you'll hear about it once we return. Over the news or at the next Orlinia Science Conference, assuming you can acquire an invitation."

Lara stared back at him. "I'm sure I will," Lara replied.

Pindrazi smiled back at her unconvincingly.

"Now, if you'll excuse us. I believe we have taken a long enough break for one morning."

"Yes, of course," Lara replied slowly making her way to the door. "Please, don't hesitate to call my husband or me if you need anything else."

Pindrazi continued to follow her over to the door, as though he was trying to herd her out. "Indeed, I shall, thank you."

Lara stepped out into the doorway, looking back one last time to see Pindrazi close the door behind her. He smiled at her mischievously through the window, as he tapped on the button on the door to fog the window.

Lara stood idly at the door for a moment, feeling an uncomfortable urge in her gut. She started making her way down the hall. She stopped.

She heard it again.

An eerie deep groan, accompanied by a chilling rhythmic scream, coming directly from the doorway behind her.

Her eyes grew wide. She turned around and stared at the doorway.

The sound stopped.

She heard the elevator doors back down the hallway open. She turned around to see Artie walking down the hallway toward her.

"Morning," he said to her.

"Shhh," she said back to him trying to listen once again.

"What?"

They both stood silently in the hallway.

"You hear that?" asked Lara.

"Hear what? If it's the circulation system, I already yelled at Patrick about it," Artie replied.

"No," Lara replied. She waited for another moment, hoping the sound would repeat with someone else to hold witness.

"What?" asked Artie listening to the gentle hum of the ship.

"I don't like whatever he's working on," said Lara.

"What do think it is?" asked Artie.

"Something alive," Lara replied.

"Joy. I'm sure he's not just going to tell us. And the more we pick at him, the more stress he will be when we get back. No reason to make a fuss over nothing. Best thing to do is leave it and him alone."

Lara sighed and glared over at him. "Fine. But if he causes us problems, you get to handle it." Lara brushed past her husband and strolled her way over to the elevator.

"Like I don't already?" said Artie to himself.

◆ ◆ ◆

"That it?" asked Cliff.

"Yea, that's it," Lem replied standing next to him, putting her welding gloves on, wearing her welding goggles over her forehead. "That heating duct runs the full length of this level. If it stays like that for another hour or so, the forward cabins on this level will all freeze."

Standing on the catwalk over the cargo containers, Lem and Cliff peered down over at the uncoupled heating vent.

"I'll climb down there first," said Lem lifting her leg over the railing.

"You what?" Cliff gawked at her as if she had suggested taking a leisure walk outside in space.

Lem straddled the railing and looked back over at him. "I'll climb down, you hand me the cutter, then jump down behind me."

Cliff moved over toward the railing. There was at least a twenty or thirty-foot drop down to the next level of the ship. All they would be standing on was a narrow row of steel pipes and tethered cables running the length of the duct.

"Yea, no. I'll stay up here," Cliff replied.

Lem hopped down onto the steel pipes and looked back up at him. "Come on. If a girl can do it, surely a beefy man like yourself can. Woman up."

Cliff stepped back out of her view and bit his lip. He picked up the cutting kit, struggling to drag it across the walk. With one mighty heave, he bent over the railing to hand it down to her, trying not to drop it. Letting go of the kit, he stood at the railing for a moment. "On one condition. I get to look at your butt on the way back up," he said down to her.

Lem placed the kit down on the pipes and looked back up at him. She thought about the arrangement for a moment. "Fine," she replied. "No touching though."

Cliff turned away and smiled so she wouldn't see.

"Are you coming?" Lem yelled back up at him.

Cliff moved back over toward the railing and looked back down once more. He lifted his leg over the railing, feeling butterflies starting to flutter in his stomach.

"Come on. The longer you make me stand here, the more I'll make you mop up the water from off the walls up front later," said Lem. "Just jump down."

Cliff hopped down onto the steel cables. The bundle shook and rumbled, causing him to slip on the rounded surface. Lem swiftly reached out and grabbed him by the rim of his pants. Cliff sat down on the pipes with a heavy thud. Lem let go and looked down at him. "Wrong way," she said to him.

"Thanks," Cliff replied holding onto the catwalk edge for support while he stood back up.

"Let's hurry up and fix this before one of us turns into Humpty Dumpty," Lem replied turning around to the broken vent. Pulling the ignitor from her work belt, she twisted the gas knobs open on the kit and reached out to the end of her torch. With a soft sputter, the torch ignited, then abruptly flashed as it died.

"Ugh! Damn it," she grunted.

"What?"

"My torch is busted, so it doesn't work half as well as it should," she replied.

Lem reached out and ignited the tip again before adjusting the knobs on each of the tanks. The tip sputtered trying to stay lit.

"What am I supposed to do up here?" asked Cliff from behind her.

Lem reached up and pulled her goggles down over her eyes. "Make sure I don't fall off of course." She leaned forward and began cutting away at the edge of the vent in a shower of sparks.

Cliff sat uncomfortably on the pipes, keeping one hand close to Lem in case she drifted over the edge.

With a loud snap, the vent fell away and crashed against the floor below. Lem leaned back and removed her goggles to inspect her work. "Not clean, but it'll do."

"Cleaner than my cuts," said Patrick walking onto the catwalk above.

Lem and Cliff looked up to see him standing over them at the railing.

"You here to observe or help?" asked Lem.

"Neither. I need to borrow your torch. We forgot to get tips while we were docked, so I'm trying to make what we have left last," Patrick replied.

"You need it now?" asked Lem removing her gloves.

"The sooner, the better," Patrick replied.

Lem wiped away the end of the tip of her cutter with her glove and stood up. "Hand us down that new vent piece while you're up there," said Lem, handing Patrick her cutting kit and torch over the railing. Patrick passed the new vent piece back down to her, seeing the pale look on Cliffs face.

"Think of it this way, only twenty-two more days of this, and you'll be back home," said Patrick down to Cliff with a grin.

Cliff looked up at him, feeling light-headed, doing his best not to look down.

Seven

May 9, 2187
– 21 Days, 17 Hours Left –

Artie wandered his way through the forward halls of the ship, looking for any new signs of wear and tear in his ever-sinking vessel. It had become a regular event to find new problems or malfunctions. He was becoming convinced they were the result of the company's cheap motivations to give the crew something else to do.

He stopped at the doorway to the atrium seeing Lara sitting alone in the dark.

"What's wrong?" he asked stepping through the doorway.

"The lights are broken," Lara replied. "Checked all the breakers, and nothing's flipped."

Artie sighed. "This ship really is a space dumpster."

Lara looked over at him with surprise. "You're admitting it finally?"

"No, I've always admitted it to myself. I'm trying not to believe it," he replied.

Lara snickered.

"I can't let Lem and Pat be right all the time. Speaking of which," Artie tapped on his watch, "Pat!"

Lara stepped further into the room and felt the ends of the orchids growing in their planter. She dipped her finger down into the soil. It was dry. "Watering system is off too. Must be the same issue," she said.

"Yea!" Patrick replied from Artie's watch.

"Lights and watering system are down in the atrium," said Artie.

"All right, I'll be there in a second. Let me finish fixing the circulator," Patrick replied.

"Make it quick," Artie replied, then ended the call.

Lara sat down on the bench and closed her eyes, enjoying the clean air. The soothing sounds of the leaves blowing in the air vents helped her mind drift in the moment. She closed her eyes, trying to take in the silence, soon to be reminded of what it felt like to step outside back home.

"What are we doing after this?"

Artie stood by in the darkness checking the computer. "After what?"

"When we've paid off what we owe?" Lara replied.

Artie sat down on the bench next to her. "I haven't thought that far ahead."

"We should try again," said Lara resting her head on his shoulder.

Artie lowered his head, feeling an urge of hesitation. He wasn't sure his heart could take another earth-shattering repeat of before. Lara could see the hesitation on his gaze.

"I know you said to forget it, but we should at least try once more," she said to him.

"Why do we need to torment ourselves again?" Artie replied.

"We agreed after you fulfilled your dream, we would come back to mine."

"If we agreed, then there's no point in asking, is there?"

Lara lifted her head up from Artie's shoulder and looked at him. "I still care what you think. Yet you seem to think it'll all just go away."

The atrium door behind them opened. Patrick stepped into the room and peered through the darkness seeing the faint silhouettes of Artie and Lara sitting on the bench. "You two getting cozy in here?"

"No, just enjoying the broken lights and dying plants," Artie replied.

"Well it can't be the sector breaker on this level because I was just down there," said Patrick.

Artie stood up from the bench, leaving Lara still waiting to hear his thoughts. She stood up and turned to him, ready to force an answer out of him. "Art?"

"One minute," Artie replied putting a finger up.

"Could just be a short in one of these-"

A heavy tremble echoed through the floor. The pots in the room shook as the hanging planters all swayed violently. A frightful twisting and scratching sound passed through the hull.

The noise dissipated, leaving a looming tension in the room.

Patrick looked up at the ceiling.

Artie and Lara did the same.

"What the hell was that?" asked Lara.

Lem and Cliff continued to sit high above the cargo bay putting the finishing touches on the vent.

"Done," said Lem. "All right, you climb back up first."

"Wait, you said I could-"

"I lied. Now hurry up and give me a hand with these tools," she said interrupting him.

Cliff stared with his mouth open at her, feeling cheated out of his end of the deal. He reached up and grabbed the upper railing, then pulled himself back up. Turning around, he looked back down at Lem and reached out for the tools. "No wonder chivalry is dead," he said down to her.

Lem sniggered and hoisted the tools up to him. "They never said women had to be chiv-"

The pipes under Lem's feet suddenly shook violently. She glanced down at her feet, then back up at Cliff with in terror.

The pipes buckled and gave way from under her. Cliff frantically reached down and grabbed her by the forearm, bracing himself with the other hand against the railing.

"AH!" Cliff cried out taking all her weight in his hand. Lem swung back and forth beneath the catwalk, bumping against the supports.

Lem looked down at the pipes as they crashed against the cargo bay floor. She reached up and grabbed his arm with her free hand. "Shit! Shit! Don't let go!"

Cliff grunted struggling to hold on to her. He pulled with all his might, dragging Lem up and over the railing onto the catwalk. He fell with his back against the railing having used all the strength. Lem crawled up from her stomach and leaned back against the railing next to him with relief.

"Wrong way," Cliff said to her catching his breath.

Artie, Lara, and Patrick looked at each other trying to piece together what might have caused the tremble. They all looked at the warning light in the room.

The lights in the hallway flickered, followed by a metallic groan of the ship.

Artie gazed at the warning light, praying it would forever remain silent.

The ship fell quiet. They all held their breath.

A high-pitched wailing sound rippled its way through the ship from the bridge.

The red warning light began to flash.

"Shit!" Artie yelled over the wailing alarm sound. He ran out into the hall with Patrick and Lara chasing after him.

Lem and Cliff sat on the catwalk, catching their breath. The lights of the ship dimmed and flickered all around them. The red warning light pierced through the dark.

"What the hell is that?" asked Cliff staring up at the warning light.

"Shit! We got to move!" Lem replied standing up and dragging him to his feet.

"Where?! What's going on?" asked Cliff.

"I don't know! Just come on!"

Cliff and Lem took off down the catwalk in a full sprint, hurrying through the maintenance doorway back to the level three corridor.

Artie pressed the call button for the elevator and waited eagerly. The ship shook from side to side. Artie grabbed hold of the elevator railing. Lara and Patrick stumbled and grabbed hold of the corridor support. The ship continued to moan with an eerie sound.

"You think it's the new engine?" asked Lara hurrying up over to Artie.

"Pat, find Lem and Cliff and get down to the engine bay," shouted Artie back at him.

"You sure, boss?" questioned Patrick.

"Just go!"

Patrick nodded to him and turned around to hurry back toward the cargo bay where Lem and Cliff were working in.

Lara and Artie stood at the elevator listening to the ship continue to groan around them.

"That doesn't sound like the engine," said Lara.

"It's not. It's the hull," said Artie.

Lara stared at him through the shifting darkness, her eyes wide with fear. The elevator doors opened. Artie and Lara hurried into the elevator and pressed the call button for the bridge.

Lem and Cliff hurried toward the main lobby of the third level just in time to see Patrick running to meet them.

"The hell's going on!" shouted Lem down to him.

Patrick stopped at the large doors to the engine bay and looked through the port hole. It was dark and undisturbed.

"I don't know!" Patrick shouted back. "Get to hydroponics and tell me what you find!"

"What are we looking for?" asked Lem.

Patrick stepped through the engine bay door and stuck his head back out through the doorway. "I don't know! You'll know it when you see it!"

Lem nodded and turned back in a hurry. Cliff stood idle, dazed by the alarm and flashing warning lights throughout the ship. "I think I'll go check on something else," he said to Lem.

Lem grabbed him by the wrist and dragged him along behind her. "Woman up and come on!"

Artie pulled the elevator doors apart as they reached the main corridor. He had no time to wait for them to open by themselves. He ran down the top deck with Lara right behind him. Slamming his hand against the bridge airlock release button, he pulled the doors apart once again with the hydraulics wheezing in agony.

Lara rushed in and sat down at her console. Artie closed the doors behind him and hurried over to his chair overlooking the full length of the ship.

"It's not coming from fuel storage!" shouted Lara checking the readings on her screen.

"Send out a distress signal to the station! Once we get this dumpster under control we're making a direct abort!" shouted Artie over the alarm.

Artie's computer screen flickered. He smacked the side of the console trying to get the picture back. The screen turned black. He shouted in frustration and hurried down to the lower level of the bridge to the secondary console. He unscrewed the covering panel and slid the cover back, exposing the vast assortment of digital gauges and readings surrounding the main computer screen in the center.

Scanning through the readings, everything appeared normal, yet the alarm continued to blare its ear-splitting cry.

"Mags one through four are running slow, but not slow enough to cause any problems!" Lara shouted down to Artie.

"Check the reserves and secondary lines!" Artie shouted back.

A reflective flash from the sun outside the window suddenly caught Lara's eye. She glanced up from her console out the observation window ahead of her.

"Art!"

Artie continued to sort through the ships readouts, searching for the slightest change.

"Art!" she shouted again.

"Pressure on mid-deck two is dropping!"

"ART!"

"What!?" Artie shouted back looking up at her.

Lara pointed out the window. Artie spun around. The color drained from his face as he approached the bridge window.

"Nothing in the sub level!" shouted Lem over the radio.

Lem continued to drag Cliff along behind her, running across the hydroponics, through mid-deck toward the life support control room. She stopped at the doorway and swung her hand out to press the airlock release button. Cliff reached out and grabbed her arm.

He called out to her. "No! Don't!"

Lem looked back at him. Cliff panted out of breath, gazing through the small window to the next room. Lem glanced back to the window.

Nothing remained of the next room. A twenty-yard-tall, and forty-yard-wide gash in the hull left the next room completely exposed to the rotating void of endless space.

Artie and Lara stared out seeing the floating debris fly out into space, flashing the sun's reflection back at them off their sleek white coating. The breach slowly began to grow, piece by piece, as the cold and frigid air escaping the ship condensed and froze the exterior hull, leaving it brittle and fragile.

"Art!" shouted Lem to her watch. "We've got a major problem! We've lost all of-"

"I know," Artie replied. "We see it too."

Small chunks of debris bounced against the observation window. Artie and Lara continued to stare, listening to the white noise of the alarm.

"Lock down all the doors," said Artie.

Lara continued to stare out the window.

"Lara!" he shouted back at her.

Lara snapped out of her vacant gaze.

"Lock down all the airlocks," said Artie.

Lara looked back down at her computer and entered her pin for the emergency airlock override. The bridge doorway behind them beeped. The deadbolts on the door locked.

Lem looked down at the door in front of her. The four deadbolts around the door spun outward. All the doorways between rooms were now under heavy lockdown, requiring a pin number to open them.

Artie continued to watch the gash in the hull break away. Lara turned the master alarm off at her console. Artie stood silently, listening to the ship echo through the hull as more pieces gradually broke away in small and large chunks.

Artie lifted his watch up to his chest with his eyes still captivated out the bridge window. "Lem, round everyone up and meet us in cargo three."

Eight

May 9, 2187
- 21 Days, 14 Hours Left -

"Ah!" shouted Cernan, limping into the cargo hold resting with one arm around Lara's shoulder and the other around his wife.

Artie watched Cernan enter the room from under the workstation he was unscrewing from the wall. "You all right, Sergeant?" he shouted over to him.

"My first injury in the service, ah!" replied Cernan.

"Airlock door crushed his leg when we locked everything down," said Lara.

Cernan sat down on the office chair near the workstation. Lara kneeled and rolled his pant leg up as his wife stood at his side. She could see where the door had nearly crushed his lower leg in half, leaving a large imprint of grease and blood around the shattered fragments now piercing his flesh. Lara cringed at the sight, finding herself underprepared.

Removing her flight jacket, she used the sleeves to tie around his thigh. Cernan shouted in pain. "Pull tight on the sleeves," said

Lara over to his wife. "We'll need to get him to the infirmary as soon as we can."

Artie dragged the metal workstation across cargo three, screeching across the floor. Everyone cringed. The doors to the cargo hold slid open. Patrick, Lem, and Cliff entered, covering their ears. Patrick hurried over to the workstation carrying a rolled piece of paper under his arm and helped Artie drag the table along toward the center of the room.

"Did you bring them?" asked Artie.

"Yea found them tucked away in the main computer cabinet. Hopefully, it'll have everything on it we need because this is the only one we have," replied Patrick, handing the rolled parchment over to Artie.

The ship trembled again, followed by the warm glow and shuddering sound of the master alarm.

"Jesus, will someone please shut that thing up!" shouted Patrick, growing irritable.

Lem reached over and grabbed a metal crate wrench off the table. She strutted over to the speaker for the alarm over the door, reached up and smashed the speaker in with a few heavy swings. She looked back at everyone, seeing no one objecting to her method.

Artie unrolled the parchment across the table. He reached over and grabbed a burned piece of metal scrap from the table, staring down at the unrolled schematic of the ship. With a single stroke, he circled the rear end of the ship, then drew a circle around the rear section of the mid-deck.

"Based on what we saw up on the bridge, the hull breach is somewhere around deck one," said Artie.

"That's right near our life support," pointed out Lem.

"Is that bad?" asked Cliff standing by idly.

"If it was called death support, then no, it wouldn't be a problem," Lem replied.

Artie circled each deck down the map. "We've lost all of cabins 1E through 1H. Though with a slight change in luck, the breach might run out of momentum by cabin 1I."

Cliff moved forward toward the table, ready to propose his plan of action. "So, we just abandon ship, right?"

"What caused it?" asked Lem from the back, disregarding Cliff's plan.

"Malfunction in the reserve storage, maybe. Could have been a blockage in the ventilation from working on it. I doubt we'll ever know," Artie replied.

Lem stared over at Artie's back, suddenly feeling a sense of guilt. She had been working well within the range of the breach knowing she had forgotten to turn off the ventilation system to save time. She sat down on the crate behind her.

Cliff looked over at Lem, reading her expression.

"What do we do then?" asked Lara.

"Assuming our distress call back to the station was sent, we should get a reply with instructions in an hour, if not longer. Until then, we stay in the cargo hold as far away from the breach as possible," replied Artie.

"What about the passengers? We can't keep Cernan down here," queried Lara.

Artie hushed at his wife, trying to think. Lara scowled at him, knowing he was going to start commanding her like a soldier at any moment.

"Pat and I will go gather what we can from the infirmary and do the best we can to patch him up down here. If he gets worse, I'm willing to risk taking him up there until we get back to the station," said Artie.

"And what if they don't get back to us?" interjected Cliff, feeling restless. "What we *should* be doing is heading for the escape pods!"

Artie crumpled the schematics in his fist and turned around. He lowered his brow, ready to force his new technician back into his place. "We can't."

"Why not?! If we abandon now, they could still send a crew out to pick us all up! I'm not just going to wait here while this piñata turns to scraps of paper mache," argued Cliff.

Artie walked over to him, inches from the tip of his nose. "There are many reasons why not. First, we are traveling through space nearly two hundred times faster than a speeding bullet. If you did escape, you would be drifting away from the station faster than they could catch up to you.

"Secondly, even if you did escape, and try to survive until you made it back to Earth, the engines on the escape pod don't have enough power to slow down.

"And finally, the life support on one of those pods can only sustain two people for a maximum of fifteen days. They were meant to be a last-ditch effort to comfort crew members. Unless we get close to a station or planet, they may as well be used as more storage."

Cliff was at a loss. He stared back at Artie, knowing he had no way of justifying his plan anymore.

Artie backed away, knowing he had made his point loud and clear. "Now, if there are no further objections, Pat and I will go get what we can from the infirmary. Lem and Cliff head to the crew quarters to gather the rest of the passengers and make sure no one else is injured, while Lara heads to cargo two to get doctor what's his name and the others. Understood?"

Everyone nodded at him, choosing not to contest their captain's plan.

"Good. Meet back here in ten minutes. If we all keep our heads, we can sail through this storm in one piece."

Lem reached over and grabbed Cliff by the sleeve, slowly dragging him along behind her as he hesitated to go anywhere.

Lara approached her husband. "Cernan's going to need me here," she said to him.

"He's not going anywhere, and his wife can look after him. We need Pindrazi and the others here with us. So, no matter how much he argues with you, make sure they all come back here."

"You and Patrick go get them then," argued Lara.

"Lara!" Artie shouted.

Cernan and his wife glanced over at them. Patrick stared for a moment, then looked back down at the schematics like he hadn't noticed.

Artie grunted at her, lowering his voice. "Just go. Meet us back here in ten minutes."

Lara ground her teeth under her lips. She still never got his answer back in the atrium, and she knew now wouldn't be the time to bring it up again. Yet the thought still weighed heavy on her mind.

"Fine," she muttered to him walking away, leaving Artie and Patrick still discussing their plan of action at the workstation.

♦ ♦ ♦

Reaching the next airlock door, Lara peered inside the reserve fuel storage room. It was dark, but she didn't see any of the ship's exterior lights shining through a breach in the hull. She tapped on the door control panel. The screen flickered in sync with the hallway lights overhead.

The pressure inside was stable, yet she still didn't feel comfortable going in. Entering the door code, the lights inside all came on. The doorway unlocked and slid open.

Treading carefully, she stepped inside. The frozen condensation on the reserve gas tanks scattered the light throughout the room. She could hear the ship still grinding and twisting all around her. She was directly underneath the breach, and she could hear it over head.

The doorway behind her slid closed and clattered as it locked shut. The lights flickered once more.

A loud burst came from behind.

Lara shrieked and turned back around. She looked up. The light over the door had burst, sprinkling glass across the floor.

Lara put her hands over her chest, feeling her heart racing. "Keep it together girl," she mumbled to herself.

She hurried over to the next door and checked the pressure. She could already see the door to the cargo hold down the hall near the elevator. A series of shadows moved around inside the fogged window.

She reached down to enter the door code.

Her mind went blank.

She stared down at the door code for what suddenly seemed like an eternity. A high-pitched cry rippled through her ears, sounding like it was coming from over her shoulder.

Lara stood with her hand on the keypad, utterly petrified.

The echoed cries grew louder in her ears, pulsating at her ear drums.

She couldn't swallow. She couldn't blink. A looming presence dwelled over her.

All at once, she spun around to see behind her.

The sounds stopped.

No one was there.

She turned back around, ready to move on and get back to the rest of the crew.

The doorway was already open.

She stood for a moment, unable to remember if she had opened the door. She stepped inside. The ship trembled underneath her. She reached over and grabbed the metal handrail next to her.

Stepping closer toward the doorway, she could no longer see any signs of movement inside. She felt a chilling wet sensation on her hand clasped around the railing. She looked down at her hand.

It was dripping with something wet and murky in low light that she had wiped off the railing. The lights flickered, giving her a swift glance.

It was blood.

Her chest grew tighter as her heart rate quickened. She took several deep heavy breaths, trying not to panic. She took a step back and abruptly fell on her back, hitting her head on the floor near the door. She felt a warm wet sensation seeping through her jacket on her back.

Lara rolled over without any hesitation. She laid on the floor in front of the cargo door. The doorway was ajar, with a thick puddle of blood pooling out into in the hallway.

She peered through the crack in the doorway. The lifeless face of Pindrazi's assistant, Annie, stared back at her. Annie's pale vacant brown eyes stared back at her. Her mouth hanging open.

Lara slid back, with her whimpers echoing through the hallway.

She stood up looking in through the doorway. Pindrazi and his other assistant, Rupert, lay face down on the floor, their shoulders both chewed and bitten into. Blood pooled around them, seeping its way out into the hall.

Lara stared at them all, clasping her hands over her mouth. She gazed further into the cargo bay. The crate Pindrazi brought onboard was now bent and cracked open. She looked back down at the floor in horror.

Mixed in with the traces of dust and dirt, she made out the bloody footprints on the culprit. Four sharp, jagged, monstrous footprints lead out from the doorway and down the hall in the opposite direction.

Lara backed away from the doorway slowly, still clasping her blood-soaked hands over her mouth as her tears trickled down her fingertips. She hurried back toward the door to the reserve storage room. Her boots were pounding on the metal floor with fright.

She stopped at the doorway and reached down to enter the code.

"EEEEEEEYEEEAAAAAAAAAAHHHH!"

Lara froze.

A haunting animal-like scream came from the hallway behind her.

A new chill in the air seeped into the core of her bones.

Her hands trembled.

She reached down frantically trying to enter the code to the doorway. The door beeped at her, giving her an error message.

"EEEEEEYEEEAAAAAAAAAAAHHHH!"

The screams were drawing closer. They were coming from the doorway now. Lara broke away from the door keypad and rushed over to her left, in between the foot-wide gap of the wall and reserve gas tanks.

She stood with her back against the frozen tank, staring at the metal wall in front of her, listening to the horrific sound of clawed footsteps entering the room. She looked to her right.

The shadowy figure flashed in the flickering lights. Its serrated outline walked on all fours. It reared back and stood up like a bear to plant its feet into the metal tank she was behind. The tank shook violently.

Lara looked away, her face pointing to the wall as she closed her eyes. Each breath came short and rapidly as she tried to stay quiet.

The creature's very presence could be felt working its way slowly around the edge of the tank. Lara could feel the wet blood and sweat on her back now frozen to the surface of the tank, holding her in place.

She couldn't move.

"*Gurgrgrgrg…*" The creature groaned as it came closer.

It was right over her left shoulder. She could smell its rotted breath melting the frost near her. She glanced over. A dark silhouette appeared on the wall in front of her. It walked on all fours before standing back up on its hind legs again. Its shadow was over seven feet tall. Its sharp claws stretched across the metal surface of the tank. Lara opened her eyes for a moment, seeing its pointed, jagged exterior coat with four fine pointed horns extending from its head in the shadow.

Lara could see its silver eyes in her mind, actively searching for her.

It was going to find her.

Lara held her breath, sensing it was but inches away.

The ground shook beneath her as it landed back on all fours.

ARRRRR!!... ARRRRR!!... ARRRRR!!...

The red warning light in the room flashed, accompanied by the loud master alarm.

Lara could hear the creature back away, then scurry back down the hallway it came from.

She waited, trembling.

Lara stepped forward away from the tank, having melted the frost with her body heat and sweat. She glanced down at the bloody footprints on the ground. It had been right next to her, only inches from finding her.

She moved forward around the tank, peeking to see down the hallway. The hallway was empty, and whatever it was, was now gone. She ran over to the keypad and frantically entered the code. The door opened. She frantically hurried back to cargo three and the others.

♦ ♦ ♦

Lara came running back into the cargo door, just in time to see Cliff and Lem walking in with the other passengers. Artie and Patrick walked in the doorway behind her, both carrying arms full of supplies from the infirmary. Patrick broke away and tapped on the control panel to turn of the master alarm again.

"Hey, what's the rush?" questioned Artie. He stared at his wife's horrified expression, noticing the blood across her chest and arms.

"Oh my God! Are you all right?" asked Lem, hurrying over to her.

"Is that blood?" asked Cliff staring at her from across the room.

One of the passengers whimpered with fright and covered her mouth. Cernan sat up in his chair, worried by the frantic atmosphere in the room. "Everyone just calm down and take a seat somewhere," he shouted at everyone else.

Artie set his supplies down on the workstation and grabbed his sobbing wife by the arm and led her over to a small stack of crates, away from the other passengers. The rest of his crew followed while Cliff stayed back, watching from a distance.

Lara sat down on the boxes, desperately trying to gather breath as she wallowed in her tears and hysteria.

"Lara, take a breath, hun. What happened? Are you hurt?" asked Artie in a calming voice.

Lem reached over and grabbed a set of bandages and cleaning pads from Patrick's arms. She bent down on one knee and started wiping the blood away from Lara's arms. "Are you cut?"

Lara shook her head, repeatedly gasping trying to take a decent breath.

"Lara, look at me!" said Artie grabbing her hands. "What happened?"

Lara's breathing finally settled. "Ther-there's something down there."

Everyone looked down at her, petrified as they listened. Cliff felt a chill run through him.

"It kill-illed Pindrazi, and Annie, an-an-and… Rupert."

Artie stared into his wife's eyes. She was telling the truth. He had never seen her this shaken up. He let go of her hand, suddenly realizing whose blood she was covered in.

"I ran, but it found me in the reserve," muttered Lara.

"What was it?" asked Patrick. "Like a dog or something?"

"No… Something worse."

The passengers at the far room all muttered in worry to themselves.

Artie instantly remembered the strange animal his wife had mentioned Pindrazi had brought with him on the ship. It had broken free.

Everyone stared at her as she continued to sob, struggling to accept what they had just heard.

"Things just got a whole lot worse," muttered Lem.

Artie stood up. Lara curled back up into a cry of terror.

"Lem, clean her up and find her a new set of clothes," commanded Artie.

Lem nodded up at him. "All right, Cap."

"Pat, and Cliff, you guys come with me."

"To where?" asked Patrick.

"We need to go see this for ourselves," Artie replied grabbing the flashlight from under the workbench.

Cliff hurried over to them. "Hell no! This is how all horror movies start. I'm not going to be the black guy that dies first! I'm staying right here with everyone else!"

Artie glared at him. He looked over at Patrick, hoping his close friend wasn't as cowardly as his new technician.

Patrick looked at Artie for a moment with a worried stare. He ground his teeth, pulled a new pack of cigarettes from his shirt pocket, then tore the pack open with his teeth before slipping a cigarette between his lips. He reached over and grabbed a bent steel conduit pipe from off the ground. "Let's go kill this bastard."

♦ ♦ ♦

Artie and Patrick trod cautiously through the ship. Patrick stayed close to Artie's side holding his pipe at the ready. Artie aimed his flashlight down the hallway ahead of them, listening carefully through the echoes of the wounded ship.

"If we find this thing, what's your plan for killing it? Unless it hates light, that flashlight's going to be as useless as tits on a boar," said Patrick.

"I don't," Artie replied.

"What?!" Patrick whispered in disbelief.

"If we find it, we get the hell away from it. All the doors are on lockdown, so it's got to be stuck at the rear end of the ship with nowhere to go. I just want to see this thing and what it's done firsthand before we lock it up."

"Well if I get the chance to beat this thing to death, I'm not hesitating," Patrick replied.

"Fine by me," said Artie.

Artie and Patrick could see the doorway to the reserve fuel storage through the next hall. Artie entered the unlock code to move on. The hallway door slid open. They stepped through, checking each shadowy corner of the hallway.

The door closed behind them and locked with the clattering of deadbolts.

"Would you back off? I can feel your heart beating against my arm," whispered Artie.

Patrick shifted over a step. "If I get grabbed, I'm leaving it to you to tell my wife and son what happened."

Artie looked over at him. "Nothing's going to happen. She would probably tell me you deserved it."

"Wouldn't surprise me if she's the one skulking around here in the dark in the first place. I often described her after we separated as a monster," Patrick replied.

Artie snickered as he continued to move forward.

Reaching the door to the fuel reserve, he could see Lara's bloody boot prints in a long frantic stride leading away from the doorway. He looked in through the airlock window. He spotted the red blood mark from Lara's back on the tank where she stood, along with the open door at the other end of the room.

He spotted the blood on the floor across the room coming from the cargo hold, fueling him to pursue his investigation further onward. "Come on," Artie said to Patrick.

The ship trembled, only this time it felt heavier than before. Artie glanced away from the window at Patrick.

"Did that one feel bigger to you?" asked Patrick.

"Shhh," said Artie, looking up at the metallic hallway ceiling. "Don't move…"

Artie stood still, listening to the ship groan.

A long, loud, drawn-out screech of bending metal filled the corridor.

"The hell is that?" wondered Patrick.

Artie's stomach sank. "Run."

"What?" asked Patrick.

"Run!" Artie yelled turning around into a full sprint toward the doorway behind them.

Patrick took off in a sprint behind him.

Artie reached the airlock and desperately started entering the door code.

"Shit, shit, open it!" yelled Patrick. He looked back. The walls of the hallway began to twist and bend in an unsettling way. The doorway to the reserve bent outward. The metal groaned and screamed around them.

Artie successfully entered the code, waiting for the door to gradually open. He wedged himself in the gap of the door and forced it open with his arms and knees.

"Come on!" he shouted back at Patrick before falling into the next room.

Patrick frantically began squeezing himself through the small gap in the doorway, as Artie started smashing the close button. The metal hall twisted until a long five-foot crack split in the outer hull wall. The escaping air pulled at Patrick's back, trying to drag him back into the hallway. Patrick clasped onto the edge of the doorway for his life, trying to pull his leg through the door.

Artie braced himself with one foot against the door. He pulled Patrick in by the arm with a fearsome shout.

The doorway closed around Patrick's boot. He pulled his foot out and collapsed onto the floor, feeling a searing pain surge up through his leg from his foot.

Artie and Patrick looked back to see his boot fly out through the breach, just as the rest of the hallway broke away into larger fragments. Through the gaping void in the hallway, they could see large chunks of debris start scattering across the rear end of the ship.

A substantial portion of the hallway dragged itself across the rear hull, pulling up more chunks of the ship before smashing into the observation window of the bridge.

Artie and Patrick stared out the airlock window from their place on the ground.

A new feeling of hopelessness overcame them.

The bridge was lost.

Nine

May 9, 2187
– 21 Days, 12 Hours Left –

Artie and Patrick walked back into cargo three with Patrick limping along, one step at a time. Lem and Cliff stood up from sitting with Lara. Cernan continued to sit back, sweating profusely from the sheer pain in his leg as his wife tried to keep his leg clean until they could perform surgery on it.

"Did you get it?" asked Cliff, eager for news.

Lem stared down at Patrick's foot as he limped along over to her. "What happened to your shoe?"

"Thankfully not attached to the rest of me," Patrick replied sitting down on a cargo crate.

Lara sat looking up at her husband as he approached, dressed in a new grey jumpsuit from the loading bay. Patrick pulled out his fresh pack of Orlinia Sweet cigarettes and put one in his mouth. Artie sat perched on the workstation and reached out toward Patrick. He snapped his fingers a few times at him.

Patrick was confused, unsure what he wanted. "I didn't know you smoked?"

Artie grabbed the pack from him and placed a cigarette between his lips before handing the pack back. Artie swept the lighter from Patrick's hand and lit the end of his cigarette, then handed it back for him to light his own.

Artie let out a deep exhale of relief in a cloud of smoke. "I haven't had one of these since recruitment," Artie replied.

"So, did you guys kill it?" asked Lem, wishing to waste no more time.

Artie looked over at her. "No."

Lara's moment of relief was stripped away. She stared at Patrick and Artie, quivering in her seat, still shaken by her memory.

"Though whatever it was, it's either dead now, or stranded at the rear end of the ship with no way to get to us. So, it shouldn't be a problem anymore," Artie added.

"What about when we need to go back there to turn the ship back around?" asked Cliff.

Artie took a deep, long drag of his cigarette. "We aren't turning around. We've got another even bigger problem now."

"What do you mean?" asked Lara.

"The bridge just became a new outdoor picnic spot," mumbled Patrick, exhaling.

"We had another breach open up before we could even get to cargo two. Part of the debris took out the bridge," said Artie.

Artie extinguished his cigarette on the metal surface of the workbench. "We are stuck back here."

"What!?" shouted Cliff.

"What about the station!?" shouted Lem standing up.

Lara sat quietly with a horrified stare. She was struck with sheer terror at the idea of spending even longer on the ship with that monster out there still. Never in her life did she want off the ship and on solid ground.

"Everyone cool it!" shouted Artie.

Cliff and Lem both fell silent.

"We are still on a free return back to Earth. Turning around and going back to the station is no longer an option. For right now, we all just need to sit tight and try and keep each other alive. When we get closer to Earth, we'll fire up the engines from the central server to slow us down, ditch the ship, and use the Schooner to get us all off the ship and over to one of the orbital docking stations."

"That's twenty-one days, Cap," said Lem.

"We've got everything we need on this half of the ship. So, if no one does anything stupid, we should be okay," Artie replied.

"What about Cernan?" wondered Lara.

Artie turned around. Cernan didn't look good. His condition had grown worse in the brief time they had spent down in the cargo bay.

"Pat?" said Artie.

"Yea, boss?" replied Patrick putting out his cigarette on the cargo floor.

"Your foot all right?"

"Yea, I'll be fine," Patrick replied rubbing his ankle.

"Good. Have someone help you carry Cernan up to the infirmary. See what the surgeon can do to help him. Lem, you go with him."

"The surgeon machine isn't capable of dealing with a wound that severe," said Lem.

"It's better than nothing. At the least it'll remove the broken fragments, and stop the bleeding so he's more comfortable until we can get him proper treatment on the station," said Artie.

Lem nodded and tapped Patrick on the shoulder. The two of them cautiously walked over to the group of passengers, ready to break the news to all of them.

Cliff stood up from his crate and started to follow them. Artie reached over and grabbed him by the forearm. "Where do you think you're going?"

"To help," Cliff replied glaring down at him.

"No. You still have a job to do around here. Get back to the central server and run a diagnostic. We are going to need it working at full capacity for when we get back," Artie replied.

"Alone? No way! I'm not going to the second floor alone! Not with that thing out there!"

"It's stuck at the rear end of the ship."

"What if it's not?" Cliff argued. "Next thing I know, it'll be using my bones to pick what's left of me out of its teeth."

"Best grow some eyes in the back of your head then. Just lock the door behind you and keep your eyes and ears open." Artie reached out and pulled his personal device out from his pocket. "Which means no using this."

Cliff reached out to grab it back from him. If there was one thing he didn't like more than his new captain, it was other people touching his personal device. "Give it back to me before I lay you out cold," said Cliff in a harsh tone.

"I'll hold on to it until you get back."

"Give it back to me, or I will not hesitate to kick your ass right here, right now…" Cliff held his hand out to him, giving him one last chance to give it back.

Artie examined the device, seeing the initials carved into the backplate:

Sgt. D.B.

Artie gave it back, sensing it obviously meant a lot more to him than he originally thought. Cliff took it from his hand and slipped it back into his pocket. He scowled at him before turning his back and walking away.

Lara continued to stare at the same bent leg of the workstation for the past three minutes. She hadn't blinked or even made a sound since Artie broke the news to her he hadn't found her new nightmare.

"Hey," Artie whispered over to her.

She continued to stare. Artie hopped up from his place on the workbench and sat down next to her. He grabbed her hand and looked at her. "Hey."

Lara looked over at him, still unoccupied in her expression.

"Hun," Artie said to her. "Everything's going to be all right. We're safe in here."

Lara started to tremble again. The dark silhouette she saw re-manifested itself in her mind. "I saw it, Art…It killed each one of them. It broke out of that crate they brought onboard."

"Was it some kind of animal?"

Lara shook her head and spoke with a sense of dread in her voice.

"No. It was a demon."

Artie watched his wife's eyes fill with fear again.

He wrapped his arms around her shoulder and laid his head on her. Lara clasped her hands around his forearm as she started to cry.

♦ ♦ ♦

Cliff rushed across the second floor toward the infirmary, eager to speak with his commanding captain. Artie stood outside the infirmary door with Lara next to him wrapped in a pale wool blanket, comforting Mrs. Cernan. They all watched through the glass window as the surgeon machine delicately rearranged the shattered fragments of Cernan's leg as he laid unconscious on the operating table.

Artie paid no attention to Cliff as he hurried up to him.

"You need to come see this," said Cliff to him out of breath.

"I'm busy at the moment, Cliff. Shouldn't you be somewhere?" Artie replied. He wasn't in the mood to deal with his new crew member, nor would he be so long as he neglected his orders.

"Your plans not going to work," Cliff replied.

"What?" Artie replied looking over at him. "There's only one captain on this ship, so unless you plan to mutiny-"

"No! I don't want to mutiny, you pirate! Just come with me."

Artie turned back to Lara and sneered. "I'll be back. Stay with her."

Cliff hurried away toward the elevator, with Artie following right behind him. Artie stepped into the elevator. "This had better be important," said Artie said to him as the elevator descended to the bottom deck.

"Believe me, if it wasn't, I wouldn't say anything," Cliff replied.

The elevator doors opened. Cliff hurried down the hall toward the doorway to the central server and ran over to the main display. Artie walked at a leisurely pace, already tired of running from place to place. Cliff tapped on the screen, waking the computer from its sleep.

Artie stood next to him, resting with his arm up on the cabinet above the computer.

Cliff typed on the keyboard and reached over to turn on the projection screen. He stepped back and swiveled the projection display toward Artie.

Artie stepped forward and examined the screen. It was a map of their trajectory taken only a few minutes ago, and there was something very wrong.

"We're going to miss Earth," said Cliff. "By a lot."

Artie pulled up the keyboard on the screen, bringing up the specs for the map. He hated to admit it, but Cliff was right. They were going to miss Earth by nearly four thousand nautical miles.

Well beyond the range of the Schooner's travel distance. And they would need to make more than one trip with all the passengers they had.

"I knew the breach had probably pushed us off course a little, but not by that much," muttered Artie.

"Did you ever shut down the oxygen to those breached compartments?" questioned Cliff.

Artie stared at the screen. Once again, Cliff was right. In all the chaos, he never shut down the ventilation to each of the compartments. They had been leaking air since the explosion, and it had pushed them well off course. Each compartment that was breached was a small burst of energy in the wrong direction.

Artie remained quiet for a moment, wishing not to admit his fault. "Can you shut them down from here?"

"Already did. Was the first thing I did when I got up here. I thought I could maybe suffocate whatever that thing is that's trapped at the back, then I bothered to check our heading."

Artie swallowed with nervousness, trying to come up with a new plan. He had nothing. To make any course corrections they would need to be on the bridge, and that was now impossible.

"Don't tell anyone about this," said Artie.

"What?"

"We can't do anything from here. We'd need to make a course correction from the bridge, which we can't do now. We'll just have to try our luck and abandon the ship early in hopes some of us will make it."

Artie tapped on the escape key on the screen. The projection disappeared.

"Couldn't we just use a spacesuit to send someone up there?" asked Cliff.

"Sure, if you want to go get one from the main airlock near the bridge?" Artie replied sarcastically.

"Why don't you? Isn't it considered humble when a Captain dies to save his crew," replied Cliff.

"I wouldn't count on me ever bothering to risk my own life to save yours."

"Maybe I should go then. Everyone would call me the hero."

"Would make my life a lot less stressful," Artie replied with a grin.

Cliff stepped toward him, ready to confront the wall that had been dividing the two of them since they first met. "What's your problem, man? Ever since I stepped on this ship, you've been nipping at me like an old dog."

"My problem is that this old dog has to deal with a young, immature pup like yourself who never listens to orders and seems to think his life is the most important!"

"I've always looked out for myself first. Always have and always will."

Artie snickered at him. "Well, in that case, I hope you enjoy your brief life living," said Artie turning his back on him.

"There's another way," said Cliff keeping his solid composure.

Artie stopped, giving him one chance to come up with a better plan.

"I can light the engine from here in the main computer compartment. Only problem is, we'd be steering blind," said Cliff.

Artie turned around, trying to keep his ill-humored expression. "If you can light the engine from here, just do the same with the navigation computer on the bridge."

"I can't. The navigation computer only relays information to the central server. It can't receive information from it, and it sends the information in waves. It's an independent system basically. DATO probably designed it for safety reasons, so no one could tamper with it from down here and crash the ship. Probably an update they added after that terrorist fiasco during the Cape incident.

Guess they couldn't lock out the main controls, so they just did what they could. If this was a new DATO model, that wouldn't be a problem, but this is an old first-generation ship."

Artie stood staring at him. "No. It's too risky. We're better off trying our chances in the Schooner."

"*But*, we could use the navigation computer in the Schooner," Cliff added.

Artie fell silent. He scratched at his beard, trying not to seem intrigued.

"I can't steer the ship with it, but it would give us a constant relay of the navigation information we need. I can input the headings and calibrations from the ship into the Schooner computer; then we can use it to help guide the ship from here over the radios. It would be like flying an airplane using a compass in the back of the plane, or driving a car from the back seat with someone up front giving you directions."

Artie walked over to the computer again and turned the projection back on. He looked down at the headings. "You'd have to make it a short burn. This ship is already carrying at max capacity. Only enough fuel to get from one station to the other, and we just lost the reserves."

Cliff read through the headings. He closed his eyes for a few seconds.

"Fifty-three seconds," said Cliff. "If I run the engines at twenty-five percent, for fifty-three seconds, I can get us back on course."

"That was quick," replied Artie. "You just make those numbers up on the spot?"

"I'm a mental calculator," Cliff replied.

"Useful," Artie replied.

"Can be."

"That's not short though. And we'd still need some fuel left over to slow down."

Cliff shrugged. "It's either that, or we pass Earth altogether."

Artie snickered at him, "All right. When we are finished in the infirmary, we'll shut down the rotation and fire up the engines."

Cliff nodded in agreement, "Fine." He spun around to the computer and started writing down the coordinates on his arm. "I'll head down to the Schooner and start calibrating the computer."

Artie began making his way out the door, back up to the infirmary. He was impressed by his new crew member's problem-solving skills, but still loathed his ego enough not to offer him another compliment.

◆ ◆ ◆

Lem sat in the cockpit chair for the Schooner with Patrick hovering over her shoulder. They both looked down at the navigation computer with Cliff standing outside the cockpit door giving them instructions.

"Just read them off to me one after the other in sequence to save time. I'll make the corrections manually and quick, so read them as fast you can, and don't get them mixed up," said Cliff to Lem and Patrick.

"I'll do the best I can," Lem replied. "I'll keep my radio on the whole time so you can hear me."

Cliff nodded in agreement.

"You sure you know what you're doing?" asked Patrick.

"Best response I've learned to give people is..." Cliff walked away, leaving Patrick and Lem with no answer.

Patrick lowered his brow in confusion. "That was comforting."

Artie waited at the door to the loading bay as Cliff walked over to him. "Everyone ready in cargo, Lara?" he asked over the radio.

"Yea, I guess," she replied.

Cliff and Artie walked back toward the central server.

"I'll need you to keep an eye on the timer for me," said Cliff.

"I'd much rather be the one flying," Artie replied.

"You can't type as fast as I can."

"It's still my ship. And if something happens and I need to take over, you better listen to my orders."

Cliff rolled his eyes out of Artie's line of sight. He had full confidence in what he was about to do, or at least he thought so.

Entering the central server hub, Artie stepped to the side of the computer console and grabbed the two loose cables they had set aside. He handed one to Cliff, then tied himself to the mounting bracket for the computer. Cliff wrapped the cord around his waist and tied it to the computer stand in front of him tightly, hoping to keep him in place while he input the changes.

Tapping on the computer screen, Cliff pulled up the manual controls and cracked his knuckles. "I'm about to steer a million-ton spacecraft through space, blind. Can't wait for that to go on my rèsumè," said Cliff.

"You pull this off, I'll give you my personal recommendation," Artie replied, bracing himself with one hand.

"Disengaging rotation," said Cliff over the radio. He tapped on the display, which emitted a subtle beep. The bottom ends of Artie's jacket started floating up over his head. He pushed them back down with his free hand and zipped his jacket. The ship grunted and groaned once more as it finally settled.

"You ready, sweet cheeks?" asked Cliff over the radio.

Lem's sigh could be heard over the radio. "Sadly, yes."

"Count it down for me," Cliff requested. "We only have one chance at this, so don't take your eyes off that clock."

"You don't have to remind me. On my mark, kid," Artie replied looking down at his watch.

Cliff took a deep breath and pulled up the ship's engine controls. The subtle humming of the ship's engines heating up could be heard throughout the ship. The ship shook with each engine firing.

"Three."

Cliff lifted his hand up and hovered his finger over the *ignition* button on the screen.

"Two."

Artie looked up and stared at the confidence in Cliff's face with one eyebrow raised.

"One."

Cliff pressed his finger firmly onto the screen. "Ignition."

The ship breathed to life with a loud gasp. Artie held on tightly, feeling the ship around him changing course. The numbers on the display for the ship's heading started to change.

"Seven, five, three, nine, nine, four, eight, five, one," said Lem over the radio.

Cliff quickly typed across the keyboard, listening carefully to Lem's call-outs.

Artie watched intently, seeing Cliff's fingers roll across the keyboard, then back up at the timer. "Fifty seconds."

"Next!" Cliff shouted frantically.

"Seven, three, eight, two, seven, four, six, five, two!"

The ship drifted heavy to one side as Cliff typed. Artie could feel each number being inputted one after the other as the changes were made. An uncomfortable feeling came over him, not being able to watch the view change out a window.

"Seven, three, three, one, six, four, six, four!"

"I'm missing one!" Cliff shouted back.

"Four!" shouted Patrick over the radio.

"Four! Shit! Sorry!" said Lem.

Cliff could feel his heart racing. Each number was life or death in endless space, and now everyone's lives were in his hands. One wrong number and they would be lost forever.

"Forty seconds," said Artie.

"Six, three, two, nine, five, six, two, two, eight!"

Artie watched the screen as their heading line updated every ten seconds. It dragged all around the screen before bending closer and closer toward the Earth. He looked over at the ship's engine readings. Something was wrong. The engines were all starting to heat up faster than normal. No doubt a side effect of the accident. "You're going to burn the engines out."

"Shhh! Again!"

"Six, eight, one, two, three, seven, three, one, four!"

The ship banked drastically toward the port side. Artie bounced off the wall, still trying to keep an eye on his watch. "Shit!" frantically yelled Cliff trying to make a correction while clutching on to the console.

"Thirty seconds! Watch the temperature," said Artie.

"Shut up and just let me drive!" Cliff replied, pulling himself back over closer to the keyboard.

"Five, three, six, two, five, eight, five, two, two! Eight I mean! The last one's eight!"

Artie could see their trajectory getting closer and closer to Earth. So, as long as they were within two hundred nautical miles, they could make it.

"Almost there, sweet cheeks! Keep going!"

"Five, six, five, five, two, nine, three, one, four!"

"Fifteen seconds!"

Artie could see that the temperatures for the engines were now well beyond the normal limit. The ship's cooling system must have taken a hit during the explosion. They wouldn't last much longer.

"Shut it down, or we'll lose the engines!" Artie shouted pointing over at the projection.

"We aren't there yet! Keep going!"

"Five, two, three, nine, eight, six, one, one, two!"

"Shut it down! That's an order!" shouted Artie.

Cliff continued to type, ignoring Artie's commands. They still needed to make up another thousand miles. He was going to have to try and compensate with the last few numbers and make his estimated corrections.

"Four, seven, three, six, one, eight, seven, seven, four!"

"Shut it down!" Artie let go of the mounting bracket and began drifting toward the screen ready to hit the *Engine Shutdown*.

"Wait, wait!" Cliff shouted at him trying to block him from shutting down the engines.

Artie reared his elbow into Cliff's left shoulder. Cliff drifted back away from the keyboard, trying to input the last digit. Artie struggled to reach the shutdown button, still tethered to the mounting bracket.

Cliff reached out and pulled himself back up to the console, shoving Artie out of the way as he fought back. He input the last digit, then pressed the shutdown command on the screen. "Engine shutdown!"

The trembling beneath everyone came to a standstill. The ship fell quiet again.

Artie reached over and stabilized himself once more using the mounting bracket.

Cliff turned toward Artie. "What the hell!?"

"I told you to shut it down! You nearly blew the engines altogether," Artie shouted back.

"We still had more than a thousand miles to make up! Had I not compensated we'd still be off by eight hundred miles!"

"If we lost those engines we would have had no way of slowing ourselves down!" Artie shouted back.

Cliff huffed in anger. He turned back to the computer.

"The engines are still intact, so you can quit your bitching," said Cliff. "Engaging rotation again."

"How close are we now?" asked Lem over the radio.

Cliff rubbed his shoulder, feeling a bruise starting to form and checked the screen. "Can't get any closer," he said with an unenthused snicker.

Artie untied himself from the mounting bracket and drifted closer to the screen. "Great…"

"What?" asked Lem and Patrick.

"We're going to slam right into it," answered Artie.

"What?" asked Lara over the radio.

"We're on a collision course," Artie replied with a heavy sigh.

Cliff reached down and started untying himself from the desk. "At least we won't miss it now."

"Can we do another burn to fix it?" asked Lem.

Cliff pulled up the ship's fuel reserves on the computer.

"We don't have enough for another burn now. We used more than we expected. We don't even have enough to slow us down all the way when we get there. If we make another correction, we'll still be going too fast," said Artie.

Everyone fell quiet. Artie pondered through his head, now faced with another challenge to overcome. "Now we have 21 days to figure it out. For right now, everyone meet back in cargo three, and we'll try to get some sleep. God knows we could all use it."

Ten

May 10, 2187
– 20 Days Left –

Artie sat with his back against the far wall where he could see everyone. The soft, low hum of the ship's internal systems still running brought a relieving feeling. The occasional low grinding sound from the air re-circulator brought some concern, but he knew it was a problem he had heard long before. His ship still held together despite her recent downfalls, showing the reliability, he saw in her that no one else seemed to acknowledge.

The low, dim lights from the cargo bay weighed heavy on his eyes. He could almost fall asleep sitting up, but he needed to stay awake a little longer until he passed the next watch off to someone else.

Patrick sat across from him at the other end of the bay resting on his sleeping bag, flipping through the photos on his personal device. He laughed to himself, watching an old video of him and his son, Rye, trying to pitch the family tent in the backyard on a windy day.

He looked away from his video to see Artie struggling to stay awake; his eyes squinted and his head drooping. Patrick stood up from his sleeping bag and quietly walked over to him, stepping gently over everyone while they tried to sleep. Artie scooted over, leaving a place for him to sit down next to him on his folded blanket.

"You hardly seem tired after everything that's happened," said Artie to him softly.

"Despite everything, I still don't get a wink of sleep while on the ship. I think it's the unsettling feeling of knowing that beneath me, under several layers of metal, there's nothing but an endless and absolute nothingness. Almost like death's frightening embrace surrounding me," Patrick replied.

"I just listen to the ship and find comfort in all the white noise. Sounds almost like a metal beach with waves."

Patrick stopped for a moment and listened to the ship. "Na, it all just sounds like grinding metal to me. The breaches have finally settled, though, from what it sounds like."

"Yea, let's hope she stays that way for another twenty days."

Artie looked down at his side to see Lara had finally fallen asleep. She had been tossing and turning for the past hour. Knowing she could sleep after the terrifying events of the day helped bring him some comfort in doing the same.

Patrick pulled out his personal device and started watching his videos again. Artie looked over, seeing the video of him and Rye struggling to hold on to their tent. Artie laughed.

"We just bought a new tent for a father-son camping trip for the weekend in the mountains. We still didn't know how to pitch it, so we tried to do it in the backyard on a windy day. Alisa said we should have waited, but of course I didn't want to listen to her," Patrick said watching the video.

"You ever manage to get it up?" asked Artie.

"No. Bent all the poles, so we never actually got to go on our trip. Was only a few weeks before Alisa and I split up, so I guess you could say I wanted to give Rye a break from all the arguing."

"All things happen for a reason I guess," Artie replied.

"Yea, I guess you could say that," Patrick replied.

Artie rubbed at his eyes and yawned.

"I'll go wake the motor mouth if you want to get some sleep. I'll probably get an hour's worth in a little bit," offered Patrick.

Artie nodded to him. "All right. Anything happens, wake me."

"Right, boss," Patrick replied standing up.

Patrick shuffled his way through the sea of sleeping passengers, noticing a few people still tossing and turning in their sleeping bags. He stopped at the other end of the room where Cliff was sleeping. He gave him a gentle kick.

"Owwww!" Cliff groaned pulling the headphones out of his ears.

"Shhhh," whispered Patrick to him. "Your turn to help take watch."

Cliff lifted his watch up to his face, rubbing his eyes. He sighed unpleasantly. "Seriously? I only got like an hour."

"Quit your whining and just get up."

Cliff grunted and rubbed his head. Patrick sat back down on his sleeping bag, continuing to observe everyone. Lem was sound asleep, snoring with a trail of drool running down her pillow. Cliff sat down next to Patrick, still trying to open his eyes.

Patrick watched him as he stretched his arms out over his head, under the impression he was just trying to get on his nerves. "Would you just sit still?"

"Sorry," Cliff replied and sat back. "I need to stretch, or I'll fall asleep again."

They both sat quietly, staring out across the cargo bay. They watched Artie take off his watch and place it on the ground next to his folded blanket bed.

"So, what's the story with captain stick in the mud?" asked Cliff.

Patrick remained quiet.

"That's cool. Don't answer. I'll just continue to sit here and stretch the rest of the time."

Artie laid down on his makeshift bed and covered himself with the blanket.

"He and his wife tried to have a baby," whispered Patrick.

Cliff immediately stopped stretching and sat back.

"When I mean tried, I guess I mean had. They had a daughter. Caitlyn, I think her name was."

Cliff looked over to see Artie shuffle around in his bed trying to get comfortable, hoping he wouldn't hear them. "What happened?" asked Cliff, watching Artie toss try to get comfortable.

"She had RSV. It's a respiratory virus that's usually common in babies. Most babies get better, but not her. Her body was too weak and she passed away at seven months old."

Cliff stared at Artie and Lara. "So, how'd they end up here?" asked Cliff.

"He was a Captain for the AEUM, wanting to join the fleet's space division originally. But after Lara became pregnant, she left her job as a foreign relations clerk, and he retired ready to stay grounded so they could both start a family together. After their daughter passed away, he convinced her to sign a shipping contract and join DATO as a way to start over so they could at least fulfill part of his dream for a few years. Now they've been out here for the past five years."

Cliff felt a sense of sympathy manifest inside him. Now knowing his new captain's true story, he somehow felt his attitude toward him sway.

"So, what's her story," asked Cliff nudging down at Lem.

Patrick snickered and laughed.

"What?" wondered Cliff.

"She's a wild card. She was an orphan that grew up in Orlinia. Packed up and moved out of her foster parent's home after they didn't agree with some of her life choices at seventeen. Worked as a grease monkey at the DATO loading docks for a few years, got promoted, had the opportunity to pick a shipping contract to work on, ended up here just over a year ago."

"And you," asked Cliff.

"There's not much to talk about when it comes to me. Let's just say this ship's been my escape. Has been for the last four years, despite some drawbacks."

"What? You kill someone?" Cliff questioned jokingly.

"No, just my marriage. Now, what's yours?" asked Patrick.

Cliff looked over at him. "I don't have a story."

Patrick sneered at him. "Well, that's a load of bullshit. Not bothering to tell your own story is just impolite under such circumstances."

Cliff sighed. "Went to Stanford for four years, got a degree in computer engineering. Was top of my class till the day I graduated."

"Wow, after all that sweet talk and running your mouth, you're a computer nerd? The icing doesn't really match the cake," Patrick replied.

"After I graduated, my brother died fighting in the Middle East. I chose to join DATO, hoping to be just as brave and adventurous as he was. Though, now I'm starting to think I just joined trying to get away from all the expectations, just like everyone else."

Patrick nodded in agreement. "Not even being in deep space seems to get you away from life's many problems."

"Seems that way," Cliff replied in a somber tone.

Patrick scanned the room. "All right, you can go back to sleep if you want, kid. I doubt I'll sleep a wink anyway."

Cliff glanced over at him. "Na. I'm already awake. I think I'll stay up."

"All right. In that case, I'm going to go check on a few things while you stay here and man the fort," said Patrick standing up. He twisted his neck and rotated his shoulders, feeling his joints crack. "Ah. You're right. That does seem to help."

Cliff nodded with a smug look.

"Keep on the watch." Patrick grinned at him and quietly made his way to the door.

Cliff sat quietly alone in the cargo bay. He pulled his personal device from his pocket and slipped one headphone into his ear. He stared down at it, looking at the name engraved on the back; *Sgt. D B.*

Sergeant Daniel Bore.

♦   ♦   ♦

Artie, Lara, Cliff, and Patrick all stood huddled around the workstation with the ship's schematics in front of them. The layout now had a new circle drawn out encompassing the reserve storage and half of the life support systems levels on the ship, all inaccessible now.

"How are the O2 systems?" asked Artie over to Lara.

"They seemed all right last I checked. The breach on life support took out the front cabin, but none of the internal systems have been affected, thankfully."

"Good, that's a change," Artie replied. "How's the engine bay?"

"Bent and buckled from the burn, but they should still light when we need them, assuming nothing else happens," Patrick replied.

"How's Cernan?"

"Out, but alive. He should be able to make it till we get back, though I doubt he'll walk again," said Lara.

Lem hurried into the cargo bay and stopped next to Artie and the others at the workstation.

"We've got a new problem," she announced to everyone.

Artie dropped his head down to his chest. "As if everything was starting to go well," said Artie. "This whole thing is becoming an old sci-fi blockbuster."

"Follow me," Lem replied.

The crew all broke away from the table, following Lem out of the cargo bay and down the hall. She stopped at the doorway to the ship's electrical systems and opened the door. Sitting down at the console, Lem pulled up the power supply specs for everyone to see on the screen.

"Now when I say problem, I mean more like an inconvenience," she added.

Everyone looked at the screen, analyzing the ship's power usage.

"What am I looking at here, Lem?" asked Artie.

"This is our current power usage right now." Lem pulled up the readings from the previous day. "See the difference?"

Artie, Patrick, and Lara scanned the screen, unable to make out what she was trying to point out. They all shook their heads.

"Ugh, we are losing power," said Lem, pointing at the screen.

"Great," Patrick replied.

"The breach must have damaged one of the power cells on decks one and two. Thankfully, we still have the ones on deck three."

"So, we don't have a problem?" questioned Artie.

"No, we now only have enough power to run the ship at full capacity for-"

"Four days," answered Cliff doing the math in his head.

"Yea," said Lem feeling rudely interrupted. "We had seven, but that burn cost us a day, and we used up two more running the ship as is."

Artie rubbed his forehead, unable to believe that their luck had now gone from bad to worse. He stared at the patch on Lem's jacket he had given her, trying to find the lighter side of their situation; there really wasn't one…

"What do we do?" questioned Cliff.

"We have to turn everything off," said Lara.

"What? We'll die! How the hell are we supposed to get air if we turn everything off?" argued Cliff.

"The air circulation system runs on the little solar energy we collect. Everything else is tied to the power system. We've got to shut everything off until we get within three days of Earth," said Artie.

"What about the heat?" asked Patrick.

"Move all the passengers back to the living quarters. That level is more insulated. The rest of us will stay in the loading dock," commanded Artie.

"Why don't we just stay in the living quarters too?" wondered Lara.

"Once the power's down, the elevator will be out, and we'll need to stay on this level in case there are any further problems. We can use the maintenance hatch to reach them anyway."

Everyone fell quiet, now forced to further alter their uncomfortable living conditions. They all understood that their lives depended on it. The decision wasn't an option.

"Okay, let's hurry this up so we can shut this place down," muttered Artie waving everyone out of the room.

♦ ♦ ♦

Lem stood at the main breaker to the electrical system with everyone else standing behind her. They had rounded up all the passengers from the cargo bay, leaving them with a radio and supplies up in the living quarters. The rest of the DATO crew had gathered all the supplies they needed from the upper living decks and were as prepared as they could be for the remainder of the journey.

"Even the rotator is going to shut down, so everyone best prepare yourselves," said Lem. "This whole ship is about to become one giant, dark, refrigerator."

Artie let out a heavy sigh. "Just do it, Lem."

"Powering down." Lem pulled down on the main breaker with a heavy thud. The lights in the electrical cabin powered down. The calming hum from the ship Artie had enjoyed soon died away, reminding him that he was now having to lose another battle with his own ship.

Lara and Patrick turned on their flashlights.

"Well, this sucks," muttered Cliff from the darkness.

Eleven

May 13, 2187
– 17 Days Left –

Lem floated weightlessly at the docking bay window at the back of the ship, staring out into the star-spotted darkness. The vibrant speckled band of the Milky Way stretched out across the faded window, seen clearer than in the darkest nights back on Earth. The warmth of the sun heated the back window to the docking bay, with the shade drawn. Lem had put on her only two flight suits, her warm nightwear, and her beige flight jacket trying to keep warm.

Lem shivered staring out the window quietly, imagining the warmth of the massive cluster of suns well beyond her reach. Her thick breath was fogging up the window, forcing her to wipe the window with her sleeve.

The doorway clattered with the sounds of someone manually opening it from the other side. Lem looked back over her left shoulder toward the door. Artie floated in and closed the door hatch behind him. She turned her attention back out the window with a sniff.

"Mind if I join you?" asked Artie, floating over toward the window. He reached out for a handlebar next to her to stop his momentum.

"Your ship, Cap. I don't mind," Lem replied, crossing her arms tighter across her chest.

Artie gazed out the window next to her, zipping his flight jacket up tighter. "This room's warmer than the others."

"The sun," Lem muttered staring out. "I manually rolled down the heat shade to help let the reflection in on the other window. Helps a little."

"Might have to all move up here in that case," Artie replied.

Lem nodded in agreement.

"God, if there's one thing I miss more than anything else, it's that feeling of the sun on your bare skin. This passing in and out of darkness causes your mind to drift," said Artie.

"I miss garlic bread," whispered Lem.

"What?"

"Garlic bread. Hot, warm, cheesy garlic bread," Lem replied.

Artie snickered glancing over at her. "Stasis dried food not filling you up all the way?"

"I've tried mixing the bread crumbs with some leftover garlic from the cheddar garlic chicken meals, but it's not the same thing. Was my first brush with the reality that there are certain things you can't replace in deep space."

"Like the ocean," said Artie.

Lem closed her eyes, picturing the soft white sand and warm tranquil blue waves in front of her. Artie looked over to see Lem close her eyes.

"Lara and I took a trip down to Miami Beach before we left, knowing we wouldn't see the ocean again for five years. Of course, it rained the whole time we were there, leaving me somewhat disappointed. But now that I think back on it, it was a moment I wouldn't mind reliving.

"The loud thundering waves rolling against the shore. The wet sand beneath my feet. The warm wind and rain." Artie took a deep breath, feeling warm thought radiate around him for a moment. "Makes me miss it all. Even the aggravated honks of city traffic would be soothing. People being people."

"Yea," Lem replied opening her eyes. "Guess you don't really miss it until it's gone."

Artie nodded.

"My first few months out, I was so... awestruck by it all. When I left, I was all enveloped in that global inflation crisis. People were arguing about the new tensions building in the Middle East. And I was still torn as to whether I should have sold my truck, or loaned it to Lara's dad to drive for the next five years till I got back.

"Now, all of it just seems frivolous. All those problems, taxes, loans, politics, all just packed into that one floating blue marble in space. Drifting endlessly until none of it will exist anymore."

"First thing I'm going to do when I get back, is go to an ice cream shop and just watch everyone. Sit in the sun, under an umbrella, sunglasses over my eyes, and enjoy all the sights and sounds. Shit, once we all make it through this, we should all go," said Artie.

"That sounds like a plan to me, Cap," Lem replied.

Lem smiled at him, then continued to stare out the window. The warm thoughts of home gradually started to fade from her mind, leaving a sense of guilt starting to once again breathe its cold breath down her back.

Lem turned away from the window and pushed herself off across the room toward the Schooner. Sliding in through the open cockpit door, she wrapped herself up in the safety blanket Velcro'ed to the pilot's seat.

Artie looked back to notice the grim expression on her face. He pushed himself away from the window over toward her in the Schooner. Artie stopped and held on to the bar above the door.

"You okay?" he asked her.

"Yea, I'm fine," Lem replied with a mellow voice.

Artie raised an eyebrow at her.

Lem sighed. "I just keep feeling like I'm the one who caused all this."

"How do you figure?" questioned Artie, propping himself against the wall with one leg.

"Cliff and I were working on the vents when the whole thing happened. And I forgot to turn off the vent before I started cutting. So, maybe a spark or something caused the explosion in the ducts. Maybe I caused everything."

Artie raised his chin, hearing his crewmate's confession. "Possible… but unlikely. You guys were downwind working on the sub vents."

"Yea, but it's still possible. And with no other explanation, which makes me the guiltiest person on the ship."

Artie nodded, unable to deny the evidence against her. He stepped back and held onto the railing on the exterior of the Schooner. "We all make mistakes, Lem. I don't trust a single person who hasn't made a mistake."

"Not one that puts everyone's lives in danger, though," she replied.

Artie reached out and pointed at the patch on her jacket. "Felix culpa."

Lem glanced down at the patch and back at him, confused how the Latin phrase could suggest anything positive coming from their current situation.

"We all get that vacation now we were originally promised once we get back," said Artie.

Lem shook her head. "That's rubbing polish on a real shitty situation."

"Okay, well what's something positive we can be thankful for?"

Lem crossed her arms tighter, clinging to the warmth of her chest trying to think. She sniffed, thinking for a moment. "We're still alive."

Artie nodded in agreement. "Most of us are at least."

Lem leaned back against the wall, trying to find the brighter sides to their tragedy. The back hatch of the small ship opened behind her. The Schooner helmet drifted out from the back wall and floated into Artie's view.

Artie pushed himself forward toward the back hatch and pulled the hatch open the rest of the way. Reaching in, he pulled out the Schooner's space suit. "Hey, I forgot this was back here."

"So did I. Could have been useful when we needed it earlier."

"Yea," Artie replied shoving the suit back into the closet. "At least we have it when we might need it now."

"Guess that's another good thing to be thankful for," muttered Lem.

"That, and whatever that thing was in the back never got the chance to reach us," Artie replied.

♦   ♦   ♦

Lara entered the living quarters' main lobby from the maintenance hatch, carrying a bundle of flight suits, tied with extra wire found in the docking bay. She spotted Cernan and his wife making their way toward the mess hall as she entered closing the hatch behind her. "How's the leg, Cernan?" asked Lara.

Cernan stopped his momentum against the mess hall door and let out a wet cough. "Fine. Nice not having to walk around on it, but does sting something fierce. Was rather kind of you guys to stop the world just for me."

"Our pleasure," Lara replied with a snicker. "I brought up some extra flight suits I found down below in case anyone is still feeling cold up here."

"Much obliged," Cernan replied. "Even in a crisis, you all never fail to put others before yourselves. It's reasons like that I know we are in good hands."

Lara smiled at him. "Thanks, Sergeant."

"Go ahead, love. I'll be right there," said Cernan's wife gently nudging his shoulder. Cernan leaned back and kissed her on the cheek before maneuvering his way into the mess hall.

Lara floated over to her. They both stared in through the doorway at her husband while he oriented himself in the room out of ear's range.

"How is he?" asked Lara.

"He's been getting worse," Cernan's wife replied. "I do what I can, but if he doesn't get to a real hospital soon…"

"How are you holding up?" asked Lara.

Mrs. Cernan stared at her husband through the doorway with a bleak stare. "I'll be fine once he's fine."

Lara placed a hand on her shoulder to comfort her. She handed her the bundle of flight suits. "We'll get him home in one piece, Lisa. You all just keep warm up here, and call us if things get worse."

"Thank you," Mrs. Cernan replied, giving Lara a quick hug.

Lara gave her a reassuring smile of comfort. She turned herself around and gave a gentle push from the wall back toward the maintenance hatch.

Lara pulled back the handle on the hatch and floated inside the small passageway before closing the hatch behind her. Down the small maintenance shaft, Lara could see the bottom floor below through the port window. She clicked on her flashlight attached to her jacket and gave herself a gentle shove off the back wall.

Thinking about her own husband, Lara once again realized Artie still had never answered her question from a few days prior. Feeling it still wasn't an appropriate time to ask him, the need to know still ached in her. She had always dreamed of having a child of her own, forming a loving bond worth dying for in life, and she still wanted to. Yet she still felt a shuddering fear dwell within her. One she had come to believe couldn't be swept away until her question was answered; could they try again? And if they did, could they ever move past what happened? Knowing she had nothing else to do, Lara decided now would be a better time than ever to ask Artie again.

Reaching the bottom of the shaft, she opened the next hatch with a loud and rusty squeak. Lara dipped her head down into the next room, still feeling paranoid from her brush with death. The second level metal hallway was completely dark, with an eerie blue glow from the frost forming on the walls.

Reaching the bottom floor, she looked back up ready to close the hatch behind her.

Out of the corner of her eye, an ominous shadow scurried across the floor and into the hallway over her shoulder. She stopped.

She felt an unsettling shiver pass through her.

"Hello?" she called out down the hallway.

She floated idly in front of the hatch, keeping her head on a swivel around her.

EEEEEEEEEEEEERRRRRRRR!! BANG!

Her eyelids grew wide. She started breathing heavily, startled by the noise.

A faint shadow in the darkness began to approach her from the hallway ahead. Its breath billowed out from its mouth in the frigid darkness.

Terrified, she pointed the flashlight on her jacket her up at it. She screamed.

It was Patrick.

Lara let out a sigh of relief.

"Jesus, Lara. Scared the living hell out of me," Patrick said to her.

Lara pointed her flashlight back down at the floor, feeling a sense of relief. "You scared the living shit out of *me*," she said to him. "What are you doing down here?"

"Was having a smoke."

"But what was that noise?" she asked.

"What? You mean this?" Patrick floated over to the doorway to the supply closet. He opened the door, then pushed off the back wall to close it again. The door squealed as it slid closed, then banged shut as it locked. "Figured I'd smoke in the supply closet to help me keep warm."

Lara let out a heavy sigh. She laughed.

Patrick laughed back at her. He grinned at her.

Still laughing at one another, Lara turned her flashlight down the hall, ready to close the hatch.

Through the window down the hall, speckled with frost, four piercing silver eyes stared back at her through the darkness in the next room.

They blinked at her, with a thick breath emanating in the window.

Her laughter abruptly halted. She started shivering in fear and staring at the window.

Patrick continued to laugh. He looked up at her seeing the sheer dismay in her stare.

"Lara?" he asked her.

"It's right there," she whispered at him, still pointing the flashlight at the far wall next to the door shaking. She couldn't move or look away.

Patrick felt a new chill fill the hall. He slowly drifted over toward Lara.

The eyes stepped back into the darkness of the window.

Patrick looked over at the window from where she was.

"Where?" he whispered to her.

"It was right there. In the window."

"*EEEHAYEEEEEAAAAAAAAAAA!*" A frightening screech echoed through the halls around them.

Lara and Patrick both looked at one another, reconfirming the frightful sound they had just heard. They both looked back at the window. Patrick raised his flashlight up to see through the window.

Bang!

The walls near the door thundered from the opposite side.

Lara and Patrick both shook, and continued to stare at the doorway.

Bang!

Another loud rumble propelled its way down the hall toward them.

Patrick trembled, sensing the urge to run. He grabbed Lara by the sleeve. "Come on!" he shouted back at her, pushing off the hatch.

They both frantically hurried their way back down the hallway toward the cargo bay, hearing the buckling trembles over the low, sinister echoes of the air blowing past them down the hall. Another loud bang came from the doorway. Patrick and Lara both reached out and began clawing their way up the walls of the ship.

"Keep going! Don't look back!" Patrick yelled over to her.

Unable to slow his momentum, Patrick slammed into the wall next to the cargo door with a loud thud. Aching in pain, he looked back to see Lara hurrying after him.

He reached out and grabbed her by the hand to slow her down. With a gentler thud, Lara stopped at the cargo door.

They both stared back down the hallway with their flashlights, ready to enter the cargo bay at any moment.

The banging stopped. The hallway remained empty.

Out of breath, they both waited, anticipating the sight of their stowaway killer around the corner.

"I think we're safe," Patrick said out of breath.

"How did it get up here?" asked Lara.

"I don't know," Patrick replied.

A faint haunting screech echoed up through the hallway, reminding them that they were now no longer the only living creatures on the second deck.

♦ ♦ ♦

Having finished their talk in the docking bay, Artie and Lem reentered the cargo bay from the rear. Patrick and Lara stood watch at the cargo bay door, still paranoid by their incident in the hallway.

"It's here!" Lara yelled across the cargo bay to Artie and Lem.

"What do you mean it's here?" asked Artie slowly making his way over to them.

"It! That thing somehow made it past the breach to this side!" Lara replied.

Artie slowed himself down as he reached them, and peered through the glass.

"You see it too, Pat?"

Patrick still watched out the window, petrified in his gaze. He looked over and nodded at Artie with a serious expression. "It's stuck in C hall, but who knows for how long. If it got past the breach…"

"All right! Everyone's required to stay here from now on unless you have to go out there," ordered Artie. "Lara, message the upper deck and let them know what's going on."

Lara pushed off from the wall and hurried over to her radio fastened to the far wall. Lem approached the door cautiously and looked out of it next to Patrick.

"Wait, where's Cliff?" asked Lem looking around.

Everyone scanned the room. Patrick pushed away from the door and over to his sleeping bag duct taped to the wall. He patted it with his hand. "He's not in his bag."

"Who last saw him?" asked Artie.

Everyone shrugged, now worried about their newest crew member.

Through the doorway window, a shadow lingered in the hallway. "There's something out there," said Lem.

Artie hurried over to the cargo door. A loud thud clattered against the door. The manual locks on the door turned very slowly. Whatever was on the other side struggled to get the door open.

Patrick reached over and pulled his taped pipe off the wall, ready to swing at whatever came in.

The door opened.

"Shit! You guys just going to stare at me through the window or you going to help me?" grumbled Cliff, drifting in through the door with his arms full of supplies.

Artie reached out and yanked Cliff inside, while Lem slammed the door shut.

"Hey!" Cliff yelled. "Watch your hands, old man!"

"Where were you?" Artie asked commandingly.

"I was collecting stuff from the server room and the maintenance closets. I think I can get the exterior boosters going again without the main power hub. I don't know about the rest of you, but I'm sick of floating around while I'm trying to sleep."

"Did you see it?" asked Lem.

"See what?" asked Cliff.

"Obviously not, if he didn't come fleeing in here like a startled coyote," said Patrick.

Cliff turned to Artie befuddled and confused.

"That thing made it to the forward deck on this level," said Artie.

Cliff's jaw dropped. He let go of his supplies as they floated freely away from him. "It what?"

Patrick raised his eyebrows at him. "You're lucky it's stuck in C hall still."

"Holy shit!" Cliff yelped brushing his hand through his curly hair, realizing how close he had possibly come to death. Artie rolled his eyes with how dramatic he was being.

"What's all this for?" asked Patrick grabbing a spool of wiring from out of the air.

Cliff looked over at him, trying to regain a grip on himself. He rubbed his forehead, trying to recall why he had gone out in the first place. "Uh, it's for a space heater. I think I can make one using one of the backup batteries from the Schooner."

Patrick stared at the spool, impressed. He tossed it back over to him. Lem backed away from the door and started helping collect the supplies again for him.

"What did you mean by, you think you can get the exterior boosters going again?" asked Artie.

Cliff recollected his things and floated over to his sleeping bag. He shuffled all his loose supplies inside, then turned back around to face everyone.

"Well, all the valves are electric, right? And they all have a fail-safe that when the ship loses power, they stop all the ship's momentum and close all together, unless there's a constant flow of power. Otherwise the ship would just end up spiraling out of control, yes?"

"Yea," Artie replied.

"If we can get one of those other backup batteries to the central server, I can use the power from the dinghy ship batteries to start up the valves again and keep them from shutting down until we turn the central system back on. I got the idea while I was down there collecting stuff."

"No, it's too risky," interrupted Artie. "Those batteries weigh a ton, and we'd need to hurry in case that thing is out there still."

Cliff scowled at him. "If it's still stuck in a hallway, what's the worry?"

"Coming from the man who didn't want to go out there when it was free before. If one of us gets between one of those batteries and a wall, we'd have four dead people on this ship."

Cliff continued to glare at his overbearing captain.

Lem wandered over next to Artie, knowing by Cliff's sheer composure that he was trying to plant a sense of bravery in himself.

"He's got a good point, Cap. If we move slowly and keep a lookout, we could have the gravity back in an hour. Might even limit how that thing can move around."

Artie glanced over at Lara. She hung idly with the radio in her hand. She shook her head at him. He turned to Patrick. Patrick had the same worried look.

"Don't make me regret this," said Artie staring at Cliff. "Lara, Pat, and Cliff, you guys and I will move the battery. Lem, you keep an eye out for us."

♦   ♦   ♦

Lem waited at the end of the hall with her flashlight; a rope tied around her waist, tethered back to the inside of the cargo bay in case she needed a quick escape.

"See anything?" asked Cliff.

Lem turned the corner and pointed her flashlight at the door. "He's not here anymore, but he sure as hell's been here."

The left wall near the door was now bent and misshapen.

"This thing's a beast! It bent the whole wall!" Lem whispered loudly back to everyone.

"Is the door still closed?" asked Patrick.

"Yea! Only just, though, by the looks of it!"

Artie turned to the rest of his crew waiting around the large dresser-sized battery in the doorway. He could see the lack of focus in everyone's eyes. "Slow and steady. Don't rush and don't push."

Lara stared off into space, almost completely absentminded.

"Lara," Artie whispered to her.

She gazed at him, already startled.

"It'll be all right. Just keep close to everyone."

Lara nodded at him, still expressing concern.

"All right, let's move."

Altogether, the crew shuffled the large battery through the doorway. Artie backed out into the hallway first, trying to keep his eyes on both the battery and the hallway. Patrick and Cliff floated out of the cargo bay alongside, both looking down through the darkness toward Lem.

Lara felt hesitant to leave. Had it not been for the slow pull of the moving cargo, she gladly would have stayed behind.

Gracefully slowing the floating battery to a halt, they rotated it to fit down the hall in the opposite direction from Lem. Cliff could see Lara's panic starting to build in the low light hall, having her back to where she had seen her nightmare.

"I can switch with you if you want?" offered Cliff to her.

Lara quickly nodded at him. She shifted her way toward him as he did the same to trade places, so she didn't feel as exposed.

Artie raised his hand to everyone and gave them the signal to start moving the battery back his way. Altogether, everyone gave a gentle push, helping guide the battery down the hall.

Lem remained vigilant, never taking her eyes off the door for a single moment. She wanted to see how the progress was going but was too terrified at what she might see if she looked away, even for a second. Yet she still had a frightening urge to see what disfigured beast dwelled beyond the airlock door ahead of her.

"EEEEEEEEEEEEEERRRRRRRRR!"

Lem could hear the faint alarming scream coming from the doorway. She stared at the door window, waiting to see something.

"It's still down here!" Lem whispered to everyone in a panic.

Everyone's hearts started to race.

"Everyone relax. Just keep moving," whispered Artie.

Lem could hear a faint thunder coming from down the hall. She continued to watch.

With a loud bang of bending metal, the far wall buckled outward toward her. Lem's face turned pale. "Holy shit!" she quietly whispered to herself.

Whatever was in there, was on the other side of the door.

Everyone at the far end could hear the bang. They all started to push a little faster.

Reaching the end of the hall, Artie braced himself to stop the battery. Cliff let go of the battery and manually turned all the locks on the door to the central server room. The doorway creaked open in the cold.

Turning the battery around, they slowly drifted in through the doorway and into place next to the bulky server at the center of the room.

"All right, now what?" asked Artie.

Cliff pointed to the mounting bracket for the server. "Find a way to attach it, so it doesn't move."

Patrick reached over and grabbed some leftover cables off the shelf. He tied the ends of them together so they would fit the width of the battery, then handed one end to Lara.

Using a flathead screwdriver, Cliff popped open the cable junction on the wall. Artie drifted his way over next to him, still unable to trust him. Cliff sorted through the color-coded wires, trying to find one correctly labeled. "Hopefully this is the right one," whispered Cliff pulling out a blue and white color-coated one. He reached in and clipped the wire in half with the wire cutters from his jacket pocket.

Lara and Patrick floated at the base of the battery, tying the ends of the cable to the edge of the server bracket frantically.

"Hand me that box," whispered Cliff, pointing to the bin floating above Artie.

Artie pushed up from the floor and drifted toward the box. "Do we have to be in here for this?"

Cliff grabbed the box and opened it. He pulled out a few wire nuts as the others all scattered around the room. "No. Once I've connected this on to the battery, that smart box next to you should light up. Once it's primed everything, all we'll need to do it flip the switch, and it'll do the rest."

"Huh," said Artie.

"It's a safety measure, so the ship doesn't spiral out of control until everyone passes out."

"I knew that just never bothered to spend much time in here," Artie whispered.

Cliff looked over at him. "How'd you even manage to go on for five years without a computer tech."

Artie glanced around the room, knowing he had been putting it off to save money on each trip. "Don't push it."

Tying on the last nut, Lara and Patrick both peered out into the hallway toward Lem, keeping an eye out.

The control box behind Artie flashed with a low powering-up noise. The lights flashed red. "It's priming," whispered Cliff.

Still watching the door, the metal wall next to Lem slowly began to creak.

"EEEEEEERRRRRRRR!"

The scream echoed once more from down the hall.

Lem looked at the wall next to her, hearing something creaking and moving on the other side.

The wall slammed and bent outward at her.

She jumped back and stared at it as the metal groaned.

A loud thunderous bang came from the doorway around the corner. Terrified, Lem crept forward and looked at the door. A faint shadow loomed in the window.

Cliff and Artie still stood at the control box, waiting for the lights.

Everything fell silent.

"EEEEEEEEEERRRRRRAAAAAAAAAAAAAAAA!!"

The door at the end of the hall burst open with an explosive bang. The airlock door crashed onto the metal deck floor.

Artie and Cliff both looked at each other hearing the explosion from down the hall.

"RUN!" Lem turned back without a moment's hesitation.

She immediately began clawing her way up the rope to the cargo bay.

Lara and Patrick both hurried their way out from the server room, neither one of them bothering to look back.

Artie grabbed Cliff by the arm and started dragging him toward the door. "No! Wait!" Cliff shouted to him, trying to break free.

The lights on the control box turned green.

Cliff reached out and flipped the toggle switch up, then turned back around to run.

The exterior boosters all fired and began spinning the ship in a circle.

Lara and Patrick hurried back to the cargo bay and turned around to see Lem clawing her way up the rope. Gradually her feet started to drift toward the ground. Lara and Patrick reach out and grabbed the rope to help pull her in.

"Come on, Lem!" shouted Patrick down to her.

Lem struggled to keep her footing as the ship rotated beneath her.

"EEEEEEERRRRRRRAAAAAAAAAAAA!!"

The screams from the hall could now be heard clearly in the doorway.

Artie and Cliff tumbled through the hall, trying to regain their footing and run back to the cargo bay.

Finally reaching the cargo bay door, Lara and Patrick reached out and pulled Lem inside by the jacket.

Artie and Cliff rushed down the hall toward everyone.

Cliff peered down the hall into the darkness before entering, seeing a faint looming shadow hurrying toward him at a frightening pace.

Patrick grabbed Cliff by the collar, and with a heavy tug, pulled him back inside as Lara slammed the door closed.

Twelve

May 16, 2187
– 14 Days, 1 hour Left –

The ship groaned and clattered, rotating through deep space toward its long-awaited destination. Three days of living in quarantine in the throat of the ship had passed, with many more to follow. Their uninvited stowaway continued to make its presence known through the chilling screams throughout the ship. The crew all remained safely locked away in their steel reinforced haven, forced to live in dark and chilling isolation.

Artie sat on the floor of the cargo bay with Lara's head in his lap as she slept. He watched everyone across the room in the artificial light, eagerly anticipating Cliff to get his space heater working.

Patrick and Cliff both stood at the workstation, continuing work on a makeshift space heater. Lem sat on the floor near the door, still listening for the creature outside.

"All right, tighten each of those for me while I finish soldering this," said Cliff to Patrick.

Patrick traded places with him and picked up the socket wrench to begin tightening each of the wire-wrapped bolts. Cliff kneeled next to the workstation. He picked up his soldering iron and began soldering the temperature circuit board to the power cable.

Watching them work, Artie's focus was swiftly broken by the sight of Lara jumping up from his lap. She looked around the room frantically, almost out of breath. A droplet of sweat trickled down her forehead.

"You okay?" asked Artie, growing concerned.

Lara looked at him and swallowed her cotton mouth with relief. "Yea... Yea, I'm all right. Every time I close my eyes, I just imagine that thing killing Pindr-"

Artie put a finger to his lips. "Best thing we can do is try to let it go. There's nothing you or I could have done."

Lara nodded to him. "I know. I just keep reminding myself. If had gone down there any sooner, I probably would have been laying alongside them."

"They brought it on themselves, Lara. Whether it was the accident that released it, or it broke out before, you and I will never know."

"What do you think it is?" asked Lara.

"I don't know. Maybe some kind of animal they were doing tests on at the station. A mountain lion, or a gorilla. I feel like I've heard the sound that thing's making from somewhere. Like at the zoo or something."

"It still out there?" asked Lara.

Artie and Lara turned toward Lem sitting on the floor. Lem glanced back and shook her head with a no. Lara sat back against the wall, feeling relieved that it had moved on to somewhere else once again. Artie stood up from under the blanket on the floor and handed it to Lara.

Lara grabbed her radio from the metal brace on the wall behind her and started sending a ping to the radio upstairs.

"When was the last time they responded?" asked Artie.

"Few hours ago. They said they could hear it up there too; then it would go away. I haven't heard a response from them since."

Artie was starting to fear the worst. Cernan and his fellow passengers on the upper deck had done an adamant job about replying to them every two hours or so. He had already lost three of his passengers and was determined he wouldn't lose anymore. "Keep trying. If we don't hear back from them soon, two of us will go up there when we know it's clear."

Lara continued to press the ping button on her radio. Artie stood up and started to make his way over toward the door. He rubbed his chest, feeling short of breath suddenly. His vision darkened for a moment. He rubbed his eyes and took a deeper breath. He crouched down next to Lem at the door and listened.

"When was the last time you heard it?" he asked her, trying to hear over Cliff and Patrick working.

Lem shrugged. "Maybe a half-hour ago."

Artie stood up and pulled the cardboard flap away from the window on the door. He peeked out into the darkness of the hallway. Nothing was there.

He coughed, seeing stars in his vision as he swayed in his step.

"You okay, Cap?" asked Lem.

Artie rubbed his eyes. "Yea. Stood up too fast."

"You ready?" asked Patrick, looking down at Cliff.

Cliff wiped his solder clean and put it away, examining his work. "Yea," he replied standing up. "Let's see if this thing works now."

Cliff flipped the toggle switch on the control. He and Patrick both waited patiently for the nickel chromium steel wires to start heating up. The cold wires gradually started to warm from grey to a soft orange. As each strand grew brighter, the space around them faded to a washed-out purple color.

"Hey! It works!" Patrick applauded.

"Huh? That's not supposed to happen," said Cliff staring at the odd purple coloration.

Artie walked over and looked at the space heater. He rubbed his chest again, trying to take deeper breaths. He stopped and stared for a minute, examining each breath as he inhaled.

"Argon."

"What?" asked Cliff looking over at him.

"Lem, shut off the circulation system," said Artie.

Lem stood up from the door. She turned to the panel behind her and powered off the air circulation.

"It's the argon. The ship's engines run on argon which is stored in the engine bay," said Artie observing the heater.

"Art, those tanks are all the way in the back," Patrick replied.

"No, but the reserve storage has backup tanks that are pumped across the ship to the engines in case of an emergency."

Lara stood up and sauntered over to the table. "Argon's not toxic or dangerous though."

"No, but if you have enough of it, it'll displace all the air," Artie replied.

"Shouldn't all the cabins be sealed off though?" quarried Cliff.

Lem rubbed at her forehead where the mark from her helmet was still healing trying to think. "All the cabins exchange air. If a vacuum is formed in a cabin, the vent is closed by the vacuum and cuts it off from everywhere else. So, unless we plan on purging the ship of all the air to seal all the vents and kill ourselves…"

"Exactly," Artie replied.

"Shit," said Cliff stepping back from the table. "So, we have to go back out there and find the leak?"

"Yes and no," said Lem. "If those tanks are on this deck, there should be a main shutoff just outside the reserve storage room just down the hall."

"How long do we have?" asked Lara.

Everyone looked over at Cliff. Cliff sighed. He gazed up, mumbling to himself. "Assuming the ship is above standard size, and it's already filled a quarter to half of this level at forty to fifty psi, probably ten to fifteen minutes before we start suffering from oxygen deprivation."

Artie could already tell his breaths were growing shorter by each passing minute. The longer they talked, the more time they were now wasting. "All right, Lem and Pat, you guys go over there and close the valve. Lara, Cliff, and I will keep an eye out for that thing."

Lem hurried over to the door and listened. "It's still gone, so if we're going to do this now's the time."

"You sure it's safe to go out there again?" asked Patrick.

"It's either you die from that thing, or you suffocate in here. You pick," Artie replied.

Patrick watched Artie walk away. "Suffocating sounds much better."

Artie slowly turned the locks on the door, trying not to make too much noise. Everyone felt hesitation to go back out. Lem clutched her radio tightly. Cliff put one of his earphones in and started playing his music softly into his ear to drown out his anxiety. Patrick lit one of his cigarettes, seeing the end glow a faint purple. He reached down to grab his steel pipe, readying himself to go back out.

The hallway was clear with obvious signs of the creature throughout the hall in the bent and protruding walls. Artie stepped out slowly and waved Lem and Patrick out after him.

Lem and Patrick hurried cautiously and quietly down the hall toward the breached reserve storage.

Lara and Cliff gradually made their way out into the hall with Artie. They all stopped in a line and stared down into the darkened hallway ahead. "Who wants to go down there first?" asked Artie.

Cliff and Lara both stared at him unenthusiastically.

"All right, we'll all go together," Artie replied.

They continued to stare at him.

"Okay, *I'll* go first."

Artie slowly worked his way down the hallway, with Lara and Cliff only a few feet from his back, scanning all around them. Lara kept her flashlight pointed ahead, listening to every subtle ping and clatter of the ship nervously. Reaching the end of the hall, they all looked around the corner slowly.

Nothing was there.

Lem and Patrick hurried to the first cabin door to the reserve storage. Lem grabbed the lever to the door and gave it a hard turn counter-clockwise. The handle wouldn't budge. She jerked at it a few more times.

"Problem?" asked Patrick holding the flashlight.

Lem grunted furiously trying to get the door open. "This door is stuck tighter than a pickle jar," Lem replied.

Lem stepped back and slammed her foot down on the end of the lever to try and work it open. The handle budged. A loud crunching sound came from the other side.

They both stood idly for a moment.

Lem pulled back on the door handle. The door resisted as small chunks of ice fell out onto the floor from inside. Opening the door, the rest of the way, Lem and Patrick both stared at the entryway in disbelief.

"Great," said Patrick in a sarcastic tone.

"Uh, Cap," said Lem into her radio.

Artie stepped back around the corner of the hallway and picked up his radio. "You guys find that shutoff yet?"

"No, Cap. It's a little more complicated than that. We've got a bigger problem now," Lem replied.

"What?" asked Artie.

"There's a wall of ice in our way," said Lem.

"A what?" Artie raised the radio closer to his ear.

Patrick grabbed the radio from Lem's hand and threw his cigarette on the ground. "An *ice-wall*," said Patrick into the radio, staring at a clear, thick layer of ice standing between them and the next room. "The pipes must have burst when we turned off the power and flooded the whole compartment."

Artie turned to Lara and Cliff. "Stay here."

Artie hurried back down the hall to the doorway, trying not to make a stir. He slid to a stop next to Patrick. He gazed at the massive wall now blocking their path.

"This has got to be at least five feet thick," said Patrick putting his hand up to the ice. "We've got to find another way around."

"There isn't one. Not anymore," said Artie.

"Do you still have my welder?" wondered Lem.

"Left it up front where I was working," Patrick replied.

"This is the only way. We don't have any time to waste looking for another. Start chopping," said Artie.

Patrick grunted and started smacking away at the ice in the doorway with his steel pipe trying to break through. Artie rushed back to the cargo bay without wasting any more time. Lem stood next to Patrick, unsure how to help. She turned around and hustled after Artie.

Stepping into the cargo bay, Artie swiftly picked up the space heater from off the table. The power cord resisted against him, reminding him it was still tethered to the heavy Schooner battery next to the workstation. He placed the heater back down and thought to himself. He glanced back at the crates lining the cargo bay and rushed over to them.

Lem ran in after him and stopped at the workstation. "Wait! We could use this!" shouted Lem over to him.

"It would take too long, and it's attached to the battery!" Artie replied, grabbing a crate wrenching tool to open each of the cargo containers.

"What's your plan then?" asked Lem running over to him.

"Don't know yet. Start cracking open these crates and tell me if you find anything useful," Artie said to her.

Splitting up, Artie and Lem one by one began opening the crates in the room. Crate after crate was filled with processed ore or broken drilling tools from the station.

"We have a ship full of drilling supplies, and yet none of it works. Ironic," Lem said, opening another crate. "They are all filled with the same thing. All except this one." Lem reached down into the crate and picked up a small, closed, white container. She read the label out loud. "Ammonium nitrate. Still of no help."

Artie lowered the lid on the crate he was opening and hurried over to her. "What did you say?"

"Ammonium nitrate. This crate is filled with bottles of it."

Artie ran back over to the crate he was opening and picked up one of the boring heads, examining the surface of it.

"Get back to Patrick and tell him to start making a hole in the wall," said Artie.

"What? Why?" asked Lem.

"Just go!" shouted Artie.

Lem scurried out the door, leaving Artie alone in the cargo bay. Artie rapidly picked up two white containers from the crate and brought them over to the table. Sweeping his arm across the table, he moved all the tools in his way onto the floor. He grabbed the blanket from his bed space and spread it out on the table over the schematics, then tore the dry lining out of his flight jacket with his hands and laid it out on top of the blanket.

He reached over and cracked open the white containers and started dusting the thick white powder inside in a line down the length of the jacket lining from sleeve to sleeve. Lem rushed back in and stared at him.

"Grab a piece of metal or something and start grinding the metal off one of those broken drilling heads. We need the metal off one ground into a bowl or something," said Artie.

Lem made her way back over to the crates and dragged a bent drilling head out and placed it on the ground next to the workstation. She ran over to the corner of the cargo bay they had stashed all their food and supplies in and picked up a clean plastic bowl to use. Artie hurried over to the designated kitchen area and grabbed the half-filled bag of salt.

"Salt?" questioned Lem.

"Yea," Artie replied. "Hopefully we'll have enough of it down here."

Lem hurried back to the drilling head and placed the bowl underneath it. She quickly began scraping the end of the boring tool with a screwdriver on the floor. The coating of metal on the tool started to chip away into a fine dusty powder into the bowl.

"Why am I doing this?" asked Lem over the low screeching sound of the screwdriver.

"You'll see here in a minute. Assuming we don't suffocate first," Artie replied pouring the salt out over top of the layer of powder. He coughed, already sensing he was running on half a lung.

Cliff and Lara continued to watch the hallway, still hearing or seeing no signs of the creature. Cliff looked back toward the cargo bay, hearing metal on metal scratching away. "The hell are they doing?" he asked over to Lara. "They're going to bring it right to us!"

Lara continued to watch, feeling her breaths start to become shorter and more drawn out. Her vision drifted, trying to keep her eyes fixed down the hallway.

"How much do you have?" asked Artie putting the bag of salt down.

"About less than half the bowl," Lem replied.

"Pass it to me then grab those zip ties from the floor."

Lem handed him the bowl of ground metal. He dusted it over the line of white powder and salt on his jacket lining, then stirred it all together with the lid from the container. He rolled the fabric up over it, then folded the ends up.

Lem handed him the zip ties. She watched as he used them to tie the rolled-up fabric closed. "Why don't you just use duct tape?"

"Can't. We need to let the water seep in." Artie picked up the roll of cloth and stood up. "Come on."

Lem followed Artie down the hall, back to where Patrick continued to chip a hole into the wall of ice. "I'm almost to the back I think," said Patrick extremely out of breath.

"Good," Artie replied. "Help me snake this thing in there."

Patrick and Artie inch by inch were working the roll of cloth into the hole that was made, struggling to push it through. "The heck is this?" asked Patrick,

"Ammonium nitrate, salt, and zinc," Artie replied. "Now hurry up and step back before we both lose our hands."

Artie, Patrick, and Lem all stepped back to the far wall away from the door. They all stood watching, waiting for something to happen, each laboring with each of breath.

"Please work. Please work," muttered Artie to himself.

The rolled-up cloth continued to remain undisturbed. The door remained frozen, with the roll of powder and fabric inside.

The condensation from the wall gradually started to seep into the warm jacket lining, wetting the powder inside. A subtle bloom of smoke appeared and started to seep its way out of the hole.

"That's going to take forever," muttered Patrick.

"Shh, give it a second," Artie replied.

The smoke faded. They all watched with anticipation in the darkness.

In a bright yellow flash, the hole in the doorway burst into a vortex of flames. The sheet of ice cracked and melted from the sudden intense heat. Artie grinned as he watched the doorway begin to melt. Patrick and Lem watched in astonishment covering their eyes from the blinding yellow aura.

The flames billowed out, leaving a charred black residue inside a now shoulder-width hole in the wall of ice.

Artie hurried over and used the jacket sleeve to brush the leftover warm residue out of the hole. He peered inside the doorway to see a way through into the next compartment.

Artie laughed. "Never thought my fascination for chemistry would ever be used like that. Help me get in."

Artie zipped up his jacket and worked his way into the hole in the way. Wiggling his shoulders, he stuck his head out into the next room, seeing the rotation in the ship had dispersed the water toward the doorway as it froze, leaving the cabin in only a thin sheet of ice.

Watching down the hallway, Lara could only see the shimmers of the frost on the walls through the broken airlock. She felt very light-headed, making it hard to distinguish anything in the darkness. Cliff sat down on the floor, coughing softly, still trying to watch for any movement.

Trying to press forward, Artie stopped, feeling his shoulders getting stuck on the ridged melted walls.

"I'm stuck!" he said back to Lem and Patrick.

Lem and Patrick both put of their hands on Artie's boots and started giving him a shove. Creeping his way along, Artie started to slide forward into the next room.

Cliff sat trying to take deeper breaths, only to come up short each time. He peered around the corner. A new shadow was now stalking the hallway. He gasped and pulled his head back.

He whispered over to Lara. "There!"

Lara looked down at him with a heavy gaze. Cliff pointed with a terrified look. Lara hesitated. She peeked around, struggling to see anything.

The nightmarish gaze of the creature reflected in her vision, as it sniffed around the hallway. She pulled her head back and waved to Cliff to start backing up.

Falling to the floor from the new hole he had made, Artie slid along the floor inside the outer cabin to the reserve storage, scanning the room for the shutoff valve. Under a thin layer of ice at the corner of the room, he could see its yellow-colored label.

"Pat, pass me your pipe for a second," said Artie, back through the hole.

Patrick handed the pipe to him. Artie cautiously worked his way over to the valve and started chiseling away at the layer of ice around it.

Cliff and Lara worked their way back toward Patrick and Lem, watching the junction in the hall closely.

"It's down there," Lara whispered.

Lem and Patrick both stuck their heads out from around the corner.

Artie brushed away the ice from the handle. He twisted the handle on the shut-off valve, and let out a sigh of relief. He walked back over to the hole and stared through to see everyone now watching around the corner.

"It's off," he said to them.

They all turned to shush him. "It's right down the hall," Cliff whispered.

Artie stood staring through the hole, listening for the sound of the creature. "Pat, stay here and help me get back through. The rest of you get back to the cargo bay and turn the circulator back on to clear the gas away."

Lara nodded and waved Lem and Cliff along. The three of them all crept their way down the hall back toward the cargo bay.

Artie shuffled his way back into the hole, with Patrick standing watch for him. Once more, his shoulders became wedged in the same space.

"Hurry up," Patrick whispered over to him.

"I'm stuck again," Artie whispered back.

Patrick hurried over to him and grabbed both of his hands. Yanking on his captain's arms, he started tugging him back through.

Reaching the cargo bay, Lara hurried over to the control panel for the circulator and flipped the switch back on. The circuits buzzed with the air starting to circulate through the floor again.

Patrick gave Artie another hard pull, dragging him out of the hole and onto the cold metal floor in front of him. Artie stood up and brushed the residue from his jacket.

A scream echoed out down through the hallway.

"EEEEEEEYAAAAAAAAAAA!"

Artie looked over at Patrick. "On the count of three, just run for the door."

Patrick nodded back at him.

Artie waited for a second and took a deep, labored breath.

"Three."

Patrick and Artie both pushed off from the wall and hurried over toward the doorway. Artie glanced down at the hallway. It was vacant, but the creature could still be heard close by, working its way toward him. Patrick hurried inside, while Lem waited at the door for them.

Artie squinted, trying to get a better look down the hall as he stopped in the doorway.

"Come on!" yelled Lem at him.

She reached out and pulled Artie back inside.

Slamming the door closed, Lem locked the door behind him. She took a now clean, fresh breath of air, resting her forehead on the door handle. She slumped down onto the floor, trying to relax. "I'm not going back out there again until we get close to home."

Artie walked over to the space heater and turned it on. The coils hummed. "We're going back out again."

Everyone fell silent. They stared over at him, waiting for the heater to warm up.

"We have to go check on everyone upstairs."

Thirteen

May 17, 2187
– 13 Days Left –

Everyone continued to gaze at Artie in disbelief as he held his hands out over the heater. They had tested fate twice, narrowly escaping each time with their lives. Now they were obligated once more to push their luck a third time.

Artie observed everyone, sensing the apparent hesitation in each one of his crew members. Cliff stood silent, with no reaction or resistance as Artie had come to expect. Lara still gazed with uncertainty, standing next to Patrick as he felt around in his pocket for his much-needed pack of cigarettes.

Artie turned back to Lem. She stood silently at the door staring at the bay floor.

"No one has anything to say?" questioned Artie.

They all stared at each other.

"I think we all knew this moment was coming," muttered Patrick. "We've been locked in here for the past week. I think we are all about ready to go take our ship back."

Artie looked over at Lara. She stared back at him. "None of us may like it, but Pat's right. We have to go check on them."

Cliff nodded with uncertainty in agreement with Lara, his voice cracking as he spoke out of nervousness. "Let's do it."

Everyone looked over at Lem, waiting for her decision on the matter.

Lem sat down on the floor next to the doorway, her hand still on the handle, staring off into space. She could still hear the faint howls of the creature out in the hallway behind her back. She was content with staying put in the bay and had finally hit a concrete wall. She was curious to see their uninvited passenger before. Now she would rather not, purely out of the fear of seeing her imagination's horrors manifested into reality. Sensing everyone's eyes on her, she decided not to disagree with them and be left in the cargo bay by herself.

"Fine," she said to everyone sounding unsure.

Artie nodded in agreement, rubbing the warmth through his hands. "Okay. We are all in agreement then. Next time that thing leaves, we'll make a break for the maintenance tunnel and check on everyone upstairs. Once we've made certain everyone's okay up there, we'll come up with a plan to deal with that thing."

◆ ◆ ◆

Artie sat next to the doorway of the cargo bay, listening carefully. He began to time when the creature came and went. It was patrolling the decks. He could hear it out in the halls for almost an hour; then it would leave for nearly 90 minutes before coming back again.

He had timed it since the first minute he heard it down on their floor, glancing at his watch intently. Without fail, the creature left within the hour, as the second deck fell silent.

"Psssst!" Artie called to everyone, starting the timer on his watch.

Patrick woke up from his nap laying back on the workstation. He reached over and picked up his now trusty steel conduit pipe. He tapped Cliff on the shoulder to wake him up.

Cliff rubbed at his eyes to see Artie waving him over. He reached down and picked up the crate jack he was using as his personal weapon.

Lara hopped up from her sleeping bag, and grabbed her wrench from the docking bay, and hurried over to the door. "It gone?"

Artie nodded to her. He reached up and pulled on the door handle gently, trying not to draw the creature back to them.

Sliding the door laterally, he looked out into the hallway with his flashlight. He didn't hear anything but the usual low groan of the frozen ship around him, ever-shifting as it rotated. He waved everyone out into the hall.

Patrick and Cliff crept out first, holding their readymade weapons and flashlights in hand. Lara followed, aiming her flashlight at the other end of the hall to watch their backs.

Artie turned back around to see Lem still sitting on her sleeping bag with her knees up to her chest. Her head rested on her knees as though she were asleep.

"Lem," he whispered over to her.

She didn't look at him. She just continued to stare into her lap with her knees up, holding another piece of steel pipe she found in the cargo bay.

"Lem, come on!"

Lem lifted her head slightly.

Artie watched her, knowing all he could do was give her a reassuring stare.

She stood up from the comfort of her sleeping bag, clutching the steel pipe tightly in her hands as she hurried over to him.

Artie searched around the door for something to use. He grabbed a strand of loose wire from building the space heater and tied it in a noose, then followed Lem out into the hallway before closing the door.

Altogether, the battered crew shuffled forward down the hall, listening carefully for any sound coming from the hallway ahead of them. They all examined the walls around them, discouraged by the sight of each of the solid steel walls now bent and mangled by some unruly force.

Patrick broke away from everyone toward the supply closet ahead. He opened the closet door with ease.

"Pat! What are you doing?" questioned Lem.

Patrick stepped into the closet and grabbed the only pack of smokes he had stored on the shelf. "Good. Son of a bitch didn't steal my last pack."

Artie snickered at him. "It probably cares about a clean sense of living."

Patrick closed the door gently, then tore the pack open with his teeth. He slipped a cigarette out from the pack between his lips. He offered one to Artie. Artie shook his head. Patrick offered one to everyone else, who all declined before he tucked the fresh pack into his pocket.

Lara reached over and pulled the cigarette from his lips. "Don't attract it," she whispered handing it back to him.

Patrick took the cigarette from her hand with a sense of thirst in his throat, then tucked it back behind his ear for later.

Together, they pressed forward toward the maintenance tunnel, checking every dark, bent corner. Reaching the end of the hall, everyone turned and looked over at the mangled doorway from which Lara had glimpsed the creature.

Turning their flashlights toward the maintenance tunnel hatch, Lara felt a sick urge fill her stomach. The hatch had been left open. She never closed it after she and Patrick fled.

"Guess that explains where it's been going," said Cliff.

Everyone approached the hatch cautiously, pointing their flashlights up into the tunnel. It was empty.

"Who's going in first?" asked Lara.

Everyone looked over at Artie. Artie looked back at his crew, feeling unloved. "Really?"

"You're the one who wanted all of us to come out here," said Lem.

"You first, Captain Confidence," muttered Cliff.

"Babies," Artie muttered, slipping his coil of wiring into his jacket. He reached up and grabbed the first bar of the ladder. Cautiously climbing each frosted step, he climbed up the ladder, half-expecting to see the startling sight of the stowaway on his ship ready to greet him at the top. Reaching the top, he pushed open the tunnel door and looked out into the living quarter's hallway.

The deck was dark and vacant. Almost too vacant for the number of passengers they had on board. A light flickered around the corner from the living corridor. He pointed the flashlight clipped to his jacket down toward the hallway the light was coming from.

A hand extended out from around the corner, frozen and lifeless. Artie hopped out of the maintenance tunnel. He turned back to everyone inside the tunnel. "Wait here for a second."

"Okay, Boss," whispered Patrick up to him.

"Why? What's up there?" whispered Cliff from down below.

Everyone hushed at him.

Artie stepped away from the tunnel and slowly crept his way over toward the corner. Lying face down on the floor was one of the workers from the station, whose name he had now forgotten. The worker's tan complexion had now faded to a chilling white, with frost beginning to form on the ends of his combed black hair.

Artie reached down and placed his hand on the man's neck. There was no pulse; just the cold of his frosted skin under his fingers.

He stepped to the side around the body and rolled the man over, checking for any bite marks.

The body was untouched. With no signs of a struggle or attack of any kind.

Artie questioned how their terrifying guest was surviving so long without food or water.

"Oh my God," whispered Lara as she and Patrick walked over.

"Is he dead?" asked Patrick.

"Yea," whispered Artie. "Has been for a little while now by the look of it."

Lem and Cliff crept over toward them, keeping their flashlights pointed down the hall searching for any movement.

Cliff bumped into Patrick's shoulder and stopped. "Sorr-" he fell silent and looked down at the floor.

Lem stopped next to him, and gasped and dropped her flashlight to the floor. Her gaze became fixed on the body lying on the ground. Cliff pointed his flashlight further down the hall ahead of everyone.

Artie stood up in unsettling disbelief.

Body after body laid spread out across the hall in the darkness. Even Cernan and his wife laid cold and lifeless at the doorway to the mess hall, side by side.

Lara gasped and clutched her hands over her mouth.

"That thing killed all of them," said Cliff from the back.

Artie stepped further into the hall and examined Cernan's body. His hand and face were a faint blue. "No. They all suffocated up here from the gas. Had it not been for your space heater, we would have ended up the same way."

Cliff felt a chill overcome him. He had accidentally saved their lives. An achievement he always wanted to live up to compared to his brother, but not in a manner he expected.

"Argon is heavy, so if it flooded this level first, the leak must have come from up here," said Artie standing back up. "Split up into groups and look for any survivors. If you come across that monster, lock it in a cabin or put an end to it before it does away with the rest of us."

"Split up?" questioned Cliff. "What is this? Scooby-Doo?"

"We have to make this quick before it heads back down to the lower level again. Last thing we need is that thing cornering us all up here," said Artie.

"There's five of us though. How are we supposed to split up?" asked Cliff.

"As you said, Scooby-Doo style. You and Lem go down C and D hall. Lara, Pat, and I will take A and B. If you find anything, use the radio."

Cliff gave him a sour stare.

"Keep on your toes, and don't let your guard down," whispered Artie to Lem and Cliff. "If you can get the jump on it, take it. If you can lock a door on it and trap it, do it. Be smart, not brave."

Lem continued to stare at the bodies throughout the corridor. Patrick, Artie, and Lara began making their way down A hallway across from the maintenance hatch.

"You guys be careful," Lara whispered back.

"Lem, come on," Cliff whispered over to her. Lem continued to stare at the bodies like a statue, void of all consciousness. Cliff shuffled his way over to her. Her eyes were watering.

"Lem," whispered Cliff again.

Lem wiped her eyes with her sleeve, already feeling the cold tear marks on her cheeks starting to freeze.

They turned away and started to work their way toward C hall, across from the now dead quarters of the ship. Cliff waded his way between the bodies across the floor, wishing not to disturb any of them. Lem followed in his tracks, doing her best not to glance down into the lifeless stares beneath her.

Reaching C hall, Cliff leaned forward and pointed his flashlight down the next corridor. It was empty, except for the body of another military passenger, lying face down. Cliff worked his way forward, clutching the flashlight in his hand tightly. Lem kept close to his heels, listening carefully for any strange sounds or movement close by.

Artie, Lara, and Patrick walked shoulder to shoulder with one another, slowly progressing their way down A hallway. They each scanned the white and blue painted crossing halls of the ship, searching for any signs of life, both friendly and unfriendly.

The hallways each appeared empty. No signs of the creature could be seen on any wall or surface, unlike the mangled interior below. Artie stopped at the infirmary and pointed his flashlight through the window.

One military passenger laid face up under the operating table, just four feet away from the medical oxygen supply masks. Artie stepped into the infirmary, leaving Patrick and Lara to continue making their way down the hall.

Stepping over toward the passenger, Artie knelt and felt for a pulse on his neck. He sighed and closed his eyes.

Artie stood back up and examined the oxygen supply cabinet. The handle was turned open, undoubtedly from the man at his feet, trying to get to clean air. Artie set his flashlight down on the metal table next to him, and pulled the sheet off the examination table, and dropped it over him.

He bowed his head, offering a moment of silence for the fellow fallen soldier.

Lara and Patrick continued to walk side by side, unaware that Artie had dropped back into the infirmary for a moment. Lara scanned her left side, approaching the first junction in the corridor bridging with B hall. She stopped at the corner and pointed her flashlight down the hall, through the cold mist.

A flicker of light flashed across the floor ahead of her. She walked over to it and bent over to pick it up. It was a white gold bracelet. She examined the bracelet, seeing it was a charm bracelet decorated with wooden charms from different cities back on earth. She pointed her flashlight toward B hall.

One of the female station workers was dead on the floor, lying on her side with one arm over her head. Lara quickly gathered where the bracelet had come from. She stepped over toward the woman, and kneeled next to her.

Carefully, she slipped the bracelet into the woman's hand and closed her finger around it. She reached up and closed the woman's eyes with her left hand, leaving her at rest on the floor.

Lara stood back up and turned around to walk back over to the corner where Patrick was.

The hallway was now empty, with no signs of Patrick or Artie anywhere. She hesitated to call out to them.

She hurried over to the corner of A hallway and pointed her flashlight down into the darkness. No one was there.

She had lost both of them.

Lem and Cliff shuffled their way down C hallway, seeing only a few signs of the creature's presence in the bent and twisted halls around them. Walking along toward D hall, Cliff felt his foot kick a small object across the floor.

He pointed his flashlight down, seeing it was a small scrap of curved metal on the floor. He turned his gaze upward, trying to find where it may have come from. To his right was a long series of metal pipes behind a safety clamp. He pointed his flashlight at them. A large jagged portion was missing from one of the pipes.

"Lem," he whispered over to her.

Lem walked over and looked at where he was pointing. "What's this pipe for?"

"This must be where the gas was leaking from," muttered Lem following where the pipe was leading with her eyes.

"Looks like something took a bite out of it," said Cliff staring at the serrated edges.

Lem observed the hole in the pipe, feeling almost certain she had seen similar marks somewhere else before.

Lara hurried her way back through A hall, scanning each of the rooms from left to right in search of either Artie or Patrick. She slid to a stop at the other end, back where they had started. She turned back around and started sprinting her way toward B hall.

She felt the urge to call out to them quietly. "Art! Pat!" she called out quietly down the hallways.

Searching helplessly, the darkness around her began to close in. Her vision started to drift, feeling her breaths become shorter and more frightened.

"Art! Pat!"

"*EEEEEEEEERRRR!*"

Lara stopped halfway down the hall, sliding on the thin frost. A shadow moved ahead of her at the T junction.

She stepped back and ducked down close to the floor near the infirmary doorway and turned off her flashlight.

Watching closely down the hall, she could see the four-legged shadow work its way down from out of the right hallway. She pulled her head back around the corner and listened carefully. The creature stomped its way down the hall and turned in her direction.

Lara closed her eyes, sensing her nightmare right around the corner from her. It sniffed precariously around the hall. It took two steps toward her. She remained still with her knees up to her chest, praying it would go away.

The creature took another step closer, still sniffing in her direction.

Lara let out a subtle whimper. She sat quietly, knowing she had blown her cover.

The steps continued but turned in the opposite direction.

Lara opened her eyes.

She could hear the creature treading its way down the hall in the opposite direction from her.

The creature let out another scream.

"EEEEERRRRRYAAAAAAAAAA!!"

Lara peeked out from around the corner to see the creature's shadow continuing down the left hall away from her.

She let out a soft sigh of relief.

She peered back around the corner again.

Four silver eyes steeped in black gazed back. Its warm breath billowed across her face.

Lara screamed.

She turned around and frantically crawled her way into the infirmary. Her cries of panic and terror filled the room.

The creature snarled behind her and crept after her.

Her shoulder crashed into the cabinet next to her, dumping all the surgical tools to the floor with a loud crash.

Lara continued to crawl.

She felt a razor-sharp claw grasp around the base of her ankle.

She flailed helplessly, grabbing onto the base of the surgical table next to her for dear life. She kicked wildly, feeling the creature's presence trying to grasp on to her and drag her away. She could hear its growls creeping into her mind, accompanied by the ear-splitting sound of a baby's cry.

"Lara!" shouted Artie's voice from off in the distance down the hall.

The creature let go.

Lara could hear it scurry away back down the hall frantically.

She looked back at her feet.

It was gone, her ankle now bleeding from the single mark where it had grabbed her.

Lara rolled over and slid across the floor with her back to the cabinets, keeping her eyes on the doorway.

"Lara!" called out Artie voice again off in the distance.

She stood up and quietly hurried toward the doorway and gazed at the junction in the hallway. The creature was gone, but its presence could still be felt close by.

"*EEEERRRYAAAAAA!*"

Lem and Cliff both looked away from the bitten gas pipe to watch their backs. The horrifying screech put them both on edge.

"It's ahead of us," muttered Cliff with a quick breath.

Lem waited for a moment, listening for any sounds of movement ahead of them.

"Come on," Lem whispered to him, walking toward D hall up ahead. They both trod cautiously, awaiting the moment they would see the creature.

Gazing over at the hallway to their left, Lem saw signs of an eerie shadow walking toward them. Lem stepped back and turned to Cliff.

"It down there?" asked Cliff.

Lem nodded. "Turn off your light and follow my lead. We'll jump it when it comes around the corner," Lem whispered.

Cliff nodded, turning off his flashlight.

Lem turned off her light and waited for her vision to adjust to the darkness. She pressed forward toward the wall next to the hallway, listening carefully.

The steps continued to move toward them, one after the other.

Cliff stood next to Lem, clutching his crate jack with both hands ready to swing. Lem held her steel pipe across her chest, ready to move the moment it crossed the corner.

The shadow crept forward just feet away from them.

Cliff shouted and swung his jack, as the shadow ducked out of the way. A hard object smashed against his collarbone, as he shouted out in pain. Lem quickly turned on her flashlight.

Patrick stood in front of them, holding his steel pipe. Cliff lay clutching at his shoulder in agony. "Shit, I thought you guys were that thing!"

"So did we," Lem replied with a sigh of relief. "Jesus! Didn't bother to use your flashlight?"

"I could have asked the same question about you two!"

"Where's Artie and Lara?" asked Lem bending down at Cliffs side.

Artie hurried toward them from down the hall, having been alerted by Cliff's shouts of agony. "What happened?"

"We got the jump on each other," Patrick replied.

Cliff fell to the floor, clutching his upper shoulder in pain. Lem unbuttoned his jacket as he tossed in anguish. "Don't move," Lem said to him.

"Where's Lara?" asked Artie.

"I lost her back at B hall. I thought she was with you," Patrick replied.

Lem pulled Cliff's jacket off and started unzipping the next one. "You didn't have to injure yourself to get me to take your clothes off."

Cliff laughed in pain, still clutching his shoulder. Lem pulled his shirt collar back and felt around his collar. Cliff ground his teeth and grunted. Lem winced in pain for him, feeling the lack of solid bone around his collar.

"Is it broke?" asked Cliff.

"Yea," Lem replied. She looked up at Artie, questioning what to do now.

Artie stood idle with a worried expression, trying to think of what to do.

Lara came running down the hall toward everyone having heard all the commotion. "It came after me," she said running toward them. Lara buried her head into Artie's chest.

"What? Are you all right?" asked Artie.

"I came looking for you, and it found me. I fought to get away from it, but it ran when it heard you coming."

Artie let out a sigh of relief seeing she was okay.

"EEEEERRRR!!"

Lara looked back down the hall where she had just come from. Everyone stared down the hall sensing an ominous presents looming nearby.

Artie's watch beeped. "We're almost out of time up here.'"

Lem closed Cliff's jacket back up to keep him warm. "Cap, we have to get him back to the cargo bay."

Patrick stepped forward toward Artie's back shoulder. "What about that thing?"

Artie stared back down into the dark hallway. It beckoned to him.

"Leave it. No one's left up here. We need to get what we can from up here and get Cliff back down the maintenance tunnel. All we can do now is cut our losses and just hunker back down like we've been doing."

Artie handed Lem the coiled-up wire from his jacket. Lem took the wire from him and wrapped it around Cliff's arm and neck to make a sling. Artie looked down at Cliff still groaning in pain on the floor, realizing the errors of his decision. He had made his first bad call, and one of his crew members had been injured because of it. Even if it was the one he liked the least.

Fourteen

May 21, 2187
– 9 Days Left –

    Resting with his back against the door, Artie could hear the creature outside on its routine pass through the lower deck of the ship. Its low roar had lost all effect on him. He had become just as accustomed to it as the rest of the ship groaning around them.

    His eyes closed for a moment. His head dropped down to his chest. The faint stench of his body odor woke him. He hadn't showered or shaved since the accident, leaving his beard wild and untamed. His hair was oily and naturally stuck back in its usual combed fashion. He fanned at his jacket, feeling the unsettling sweat building from his fever.

    Lara warmed a pot of water over the space heater next to Lem and Cliff, changing the bandage around her ankle as she waited for the water to boil. Her makeup had now faded entirely, while her pale lips still shivered next to the heater in front of her. She had hardly moved in the past five days, having only gotten up to eat or tend to her own needs.

Lem stayed curled up in a blanket on the floor next to Cliff. She continued to read a book for the second time that she had found in one of the station worker's personal things. Her eyes felt heavy, yet every time she closed her eyes to sleep, she would wake up only a few minutes later, wide awake.

Cliff rolled over on his side, and let out a painful groan of agony. Lem closed her book around the edge of her blanket and leaned forward to roll Cliff back over flat on the floor. Watching Cliff breathe with relief, she leaned back again and reopened her book.

Cliff had done nothing but sleep, either passing out from the pulsing pain in his collar or from the drowsiness of the pain medication, he continued to take.

Patrick wandered the cargo bay throughout the day, obviously deep in thought. He hardly spoke to anyone, muttering to himself with each pass of the room, adrift in his reality. He would stop every thirty minutes and watch the seconds on his watch pass.

Lara glanced over at Artie, seeing him sway in his sleep. She placed the used tea bag into the pot of water, then stood up from her place next to the space heater. She bent over and felt the top of her husband's head. His forehead was almost as warm as the space heater.

She grabbed the empty cup from off the floor next to him and poured the tea into it.

"Art, drink," she said to him, handing him the cup.

Artie stared at the cup for a moment, feeling no urge to drink anything.

"Art!"

"He doesn't have to drink it," said Patrick pacing his way past both of them.

"He's running a fever."

"So am I, but you don't hear me complaining about it," said Patrick. He reached into his pocket and pulled out his pack of smokes. The pack was empty. In an anger-filled pitch, he chucked the empty carton across the room at the workstation with an irritated growl.

Putting his hands at his side, he ran his foot into the edge of the workstation, sending a shock of pain up through his leg.
With an infuriated yell, he drilled his foot into the workstation again, flipping the table over on its side.

Artie's eyes opened to see Patrick kicking the table over with a loud bang on the steel floor.

Artie hopped up from his place on the floor and rushed over to Patrick. He grabbed him by the collar and slammed him into the full metal crate behind him. Artie glared at him through his pale, sickly stare. "You lose your temper like that again, and you'll bring that thing right to us."

"If it's going to kill us all, it should just get it over with," Patrick replied, not bothering to fight back.

"So, what? You run yourself out of smokes, and you decide life's not worth living anymore?"

"It knows we are in here. It's probably already trying to find its way into us right now."

"The only animal in here right now is you," Artie replied letting go of Patrick.

"At least I'm not the one who let twelve people die under my protection."

Artie reached out to grab him again.

Lara hurried over and stepped in between the two of them. "Hey! You're just as much to blame here as any of us. This ship is as much under our care as it is yours. Maybe if you had stopped smoking so much, you could have done your job better."

Patrick reached forward and grabbed Lara by the arm. Artie drove his arm down on top of Patrick's forearm, and slammed his fist into Patrick's stomach. Patrick immediately swung back, hitting Artie in the rib cage.

Lem rushed to her feet and ran over to both of them. She threw her body in the way, separating the two men from one another.

"Hey! Hey! Both of you cut the shit! You're both just going at each other's throats for no reason now!"

Artie stepped back and put his hand on his ribs as he coughed. Patrick threw his hands up in frustration and turned his back to everyone.

"I'm already taking care of one injured person over there, and I'm not taking care of two more. So, if you both are just going to kill each other right here and right now, we should just open the door and let that thing come in and finish all of us off. Because like it or not, this ship's not making it home without all of us."

Artie took a deep breath and reached out for Lara to help support him. Patrick lowered his arms, continuing to stare at the cargo bay doors. "Let it come then," muttered Patrick.

Lem dropped her guard, watching Artie and Patrick still holding a grudge against each other. "You want to know who the real monsters are? When I was a little kid, growing up in the orphanage, my friend Shari and I used to always be afraid of what we thought was a monster living under our bunkbed, scratching and clawing at the wall at night. When we got older, we both realized it was nothing but a mouse burrowing a den in the wall behind our bed. Back then we started to think monsters really didn't exist.

"A few years later, when we both turned sixteen, a police officer and legal official came to the orphanage, claiming we had both aged out of the orphanage, and dragged us both out onto the streets by the hair, kicking and screaming.

"The orphanage owner, Mr. Penjer, worked day and night trying to find both of us a foster family to temporarily stay with while we slept outside on the curb. A few days later, I went to a foster home he had found for me. When I arrived, the parents there had us all sleeping in sleeping bags down in the basement, and fed us out of cans while they went out to dinner every night. About a week later, they found me and one of the other girls sleeping in the same sleeping bag together, and dragged me upstairs to lecture me about how I didn't know any better, and how I was just an adolescent teenager in need of correction. Once they finished lecturing me, I packed up my things and waited till everyone was asleep.

"I never went back, and I never saw my friend Shari again. But the one thing I did learn that night was that monsters do exist. Ones that wear the skin of people believing that what they are doing is good or are doing what they are told without question, thinking it's for everyone's good. People who tear each other apart over closed-mindedness. People beating one another because they don't bother to see the world from the other person's point of view. Out of selfishness. Out of pride. Out of hatred.

"We might have lost everyone out here, but at least the five of us are still here. Like it or not, we are a crew. One which has become a family over the past seventeen days. And as a family, we should be looking out for one another, not turning into monsters ourselves."

Lem felt an emotional weight build up in her chest. She struggled to speak.

"Growing up without a family... you guys have become the closest thing I've got, and I don't intend to let the only family I've ever had start to tear itself apart from the inside out. So... you two need to put your panties back on and act like the two-humble gentlemen I know you to be and leave the monsters out there where they belong."

Patrick lowered his head in shame. He threw his hands down to his sides and walked away to his corner of the cargo bay without another word.

Artie let go of his side and lifted his arm away from Lara to stand on his own feet. Lem watched Patrick walk away, knowing her point had been made.
She wandered over toward Artie and Lara, afraid to look either of them in the eye.

"You trying to mutiny?" asked Artie.

"No, just figured my Captain could just use a good kick in the ass before he starts acting like one," Lem replied.

Artie laughed and clutched his side again. "Thanks, Lem."

He reached out and patted her on the side. "I have no doubts in my mind now, with an attitude like that, you'll make one worthy captain. Better than me most likely."

Lem gave him a slight smile. Cliff groaned and rolled over in his sleeping bag once again. She hurried back over to him, leaving Artie and Lara alone.

"You didn't need to intervene," Artie whispered to Lara.

"He's wrong. We are all to blame," argued Lara.

"No, he's right. I was responsible for all of them. They were my burden to carry. I failed, and now I'll have to live with that."

Artie coughed and winced in pain.

"You're doing it again," said Lara feeling his head once again.

"What?"

"Your puppy pout face," Lara replied.

Artie snickered at her.

"You need sleep."

Artie covered his mouth with his jacket and coughed. "I'll sleep when I make sure the rest of us make it home safely."

Fifteen

May 26, 2187
- 4 Days Left -

Lem tied the two ends of Cliff's flight jacket around the back of his neck. He let out a subtle grunt of pain. His arm swayed in the sling.

"Better?"

Cliff looked down at his arm wincing with discomfort. "Better than before, but still hurts."

He examined the patch on her jacket sleeve, admiring the intricacy. He reached out with his good arm and pointed at it. "What's that from?"

"A friend gave it to me. Means happy-"

"Happy accident? Yea, I've heard the term before. Don't see it being really relevant in this shit show though."

"Well, that's the beauty of it I guess. You never really know what's happy about it until it's all over." Lem turned around and started walking toward the others.

Cliff cleared his throat. "Hey, sweet cheeks. Thank you for taking care of me by the way."

Lem spun back around and stared at him through her bangs. "You're welcome," she replied. She stepped forward and kissed him on the cheek. Cliff grinned at her as she stepped away.

"You're still an asshole, but at least you're an asshole I don't mind having around now," said Lem, stepping backward away from him.

"That means I might have a chance to convince you to change teams?" asked Cliff.

Lem snickered. "Not on your life."

Cliff exhaled and laughed as she turned back around and walked away from him with a sense of pride in her stride. He followed her over to Artie and Lara standing by the cargo bay door. Patrick remained on his side of the room, watching Artie getting ready to make his run for the central server again to restart the ship.

"It just left, so if you're going to do it, now's the time," said Lara, watching the time on her watch.

"All right," Artie replied, taking a deep breath with a heavy cough. He was ready to bring life back into his ship, ending their nights of shivering in the refrigerated vessel and huddling together for warmth.

"Art, maybe I should go," argued Lara.

"I've said no, I mean no, and I stand by it; No. No one else needs to risk themselves for my ship when you're all my responsibility," Artie argued back, stretching out his arms.

Cliff stood next to Lem, watching Artie mentally prepare himself. "When you get there, just hit the red power prime button twice, and when you see the blue lights on the panel in front of you all light up, hit the hard restart button. It's like starting up an engine, so you'll have to prime or choke it first."

Artie nodded to him, trying to remember his instructions. Lem put her hand on Artie's shoulder. "You sure you don't want me to go, Cap?"

Artie turned the lock on the cargo door and opened it. He peeked his head out into the hall, seeing that the coast was clear. Stepping out, he turned back to look at everyone. He then closed the door behind him without saying anything, wishing not to discuss the matter any further.

Lara sneered, "I'm starting to think he enjoys theatrics."

Artie clicked his flashlight on and pressed forward down the shimmering frost-covered corridor. He panned his flashlight around behind him, keeping an eye on his back. Everything was quiet, thankfully, although the silence was starting to become unsettling for him.

He approached the door to the central server control room. With a hard yank, the thin built-up ice on the doorway broke free and crumbled to the floor. Artie stopped for a moment and peered back down the hallway next to him to make sure the coast was still clear.

His presence continued to go unnoticed. He turned his attention back to the door in front of him and opened it slowly.

Stepping inside, he closed the door behind him and began his search around the room. Finding the red priming button, he wasted no time. He started pressing the priming button, unable to recall if it was two pushes or three. He pressed the button an extra third time just to be sure and waited for the blue lights on the panel in front of him to light up. One by one, they all illuminated, until the green hard restart button flashed at his waist.

Holding his finger over the button, he prepared himself. There was no telling what effects their prolonged travel without power had taken on the ship. Artie tried to imagine the worst possible situations but knew in the end; he would never be fully prepared.

He pressed the start button, hearing the server start to buzz and hum. The lights in the room each flickered and flashed. He held his breath, waiting eagerly. The lights turned on.

Artie let out a sigh of relief, just as the lights all went dark again. The server let out a horrible, loud, buzzing noise, which echoed across the deck.

His cover was blown. Artie opened the door again and hurried his way down the hall back to the cargo bay. He knocked on the door frantically, feeling an ominous aura now creeping its way toward him from down the hall.

Artie pounded on the door rapidly.

Lem opened the locked door and pulled it open in time to see Artie fall onto the floor inside. She immediately closed the door behind him and locked it again.

"What happened?" asked Cliff.

"I don't know. I started it, but nothing happened," Artie replied, standing back up.

The cabin control panel next to them started to flash red and white with a warning reading on the display. The red warning lights outside in the hallway all began flashing with the master alarm.

WARNING:
ERROR 02700410
MANUAL MC REQUIRED

The screen flashed once more to another warning.

WARNING:
ERROR 02700369
OC AND LS SYSTEMS OFFLINE

"Shit," muttered Cliff looking at the screen. "The restart tripped the bridge's control systems. Now the life support system is offline." Cliff pressed the off button on the control panel, silencing the lights and alarm.

Lara walked away from the screen in disbelief at their luck.

"How long would you say we have to restart them?" questioned Artie.

Cliff closed his eyes for a moment and ran through the calculations in his head. "Maybe… an hour and sixteen minutes. Possibly an hour and twenty-seven if there are no leaks on this deck to any of the others."

Artie hurried over to the workstation. He picked up the schematics cylinder from off the floor and rolled back out the map of the ship's schematics and thumbed through it. He coughed into his forearm, struggling to hold the schematics out on the table.

"How do we get up to life support?" asked Lara. "That compartment's breached, and the elevator won't work until the power's back."

Artie ran his finger along the elevator shaft on the schematic. "We shut down the rotator again and float up through the elevator shaft. I'll go to the bridge, while someone else heads for life support. Assuming at least the forward half of the life support control isn't breached, that person can then restart the system once I restart the main bridge controls."

"I'll go," said Patrick walking over from his solitude in the corner of the room.

Artie glanced over at him.

"*I'll* go," Lem replied. "I can make my way up to life support, then hurry back down here once I'm done."

Artie nodded in agreement with her. Patrick shook his head with an annoyed expression approaching the workstation. "You deaf, Art? I said I'll go."

"I have full confidence that Lem can do it. You and Lara stay down here with Cliff. If the main server throws another tantrum or we have another mechanical problem down here, I can trust you to take care of it. Besides, Cliff's going to need your guys' help."

"Consider it punishment for breaking my collarbone," Cliff mumbled under his breath.

Patrick glared at him.

"How are you going to get up to the bridge? We don't have any suits down here," said Lara.

"We still have the one from the Schooner. It only has two hours' worth of air, but it'll work. I'll use it to get up there and come back down the same way," Artie replied.

Lara rubbed her forehead, not liking her husband's plan. "I'd argue you with you about it, but I know you'll just ignore everything I say and go anyway."

"What about that thing?" asked Lem.

"We don't really have a choice. Either we all die in here together, or we make our final push to survive now and clear this obstacle in our way," Artie replied.

He looked around at everyone. Through the rugged, tired stares of his crew members, Artie could see his battle-hardened crew ready to take on another challenge. They had all come so far, and with only four days left until home, they now had nothing left to fear.

"I'm ready to be home," said Lara.

"Me too," Cliff replied.

"And me," muttered Patrick.

Everyone turned their attention toward Lem. Lem closed her eyes and smiled with a face of satisfaction. "Garlic bread…"

Everyone snickered at her response.

Artie slicked his hair back from his view and zipped up his jacket the rest of the way. "All right. Let's get this ship home."

♦ ♦ ♦

Keeping a close eye on her watch, Lara made the last-minute adjustments to Artie's space suit regulator. She lifted the helmet off the floor and began slipping it over his head. She stopped and lifted it back up.

She leaned in and kissed him on the lips. "Come back, or I'll kill you myself," she muttered to him. She leaned forward and gave him another kiss. She slipped the helmet the rest of the way on and locked his helmet into place.

Artie took a few deep breaths of the clean air in his helmet, adjusting himself to the change. He raised his hand up to cough, realizing he could no longer cover his mouth. "You guys ready?"

Cliff gave him a thumbs up with his good arm. Patrick waited at the door, ready to open the way for Artie and Lem before following Cliff and Lara to the central server control room.

Lara helped Artie to his feet with both hands. He shuffled his way in the space suit over toward the door, ready to go.

"Hey, boss," said Patrick.

Artie stopped and looked over at him.

"I'm sorry."

Artie put a hand on Patrick's shoulder. "You should be."

Patrick snickered and turned his attention back to the door. He turned the lock counter-clockwise and opened the door slowly. Artie stepped out first, turning on the faint blue flashlights on his suit to see down the hallway. Lem followed Artie out, keeping her eyes out behind her while staying within arm's reach of Artie leading the way.

Patrick, Cliff, and Lara moved in the opposite direction, staying close together and watching each other's backs. Lem watched them walk away slowly, until they turned the corner where she lost sight of them.

"I don't hear anything," whispered Lem.

Artie peeked around the corner, knowing they had to go through the door the creature had broken open.

He pressed forward, feeling behind him to make sure Lem was still following. Looking down at his feet, he stopped for a moment.

"What?" asked Lem, bumping into him.

Artie looked at the base of the bent wall next to them. Two large chunks of ice rested frozen to the floor at the base of a breach in the wall, much too far away from the frozen doorway and corridor on the opposite side of them.

"Nothing," Artie replied and pressed forward.

He turned left at the corner after the broken doorway. The elevator was straight ahead, with nothing between them but the dark frosted hallway.

"We're in the elevator," Artie spoke into his radio.

"Okay, flip the toggle switch down, and wait until I say so to hit that power button," said Cliff over to Lara standing in front of the control box and Schooner battery.

Lara flipped the switch and rested her finger on the power button. Patrick stayed at the door, keeping an eye out for the creature.

The control box ticked, as all the green lights turned off all at once. "Powering down in three, two, one," said Cliff into the radio. "Now."

Lara pressed down on the black power button. The control box ticked and powered down. The ship's boosters all burst to life, slowing the ship's rotation to a halt. The false gravity around everyone disappeared, leaving them holding on to the closest handle or tethered object. Cliff grabbed hold of the rack next to him with his good arm, while Patrick held tight onto the door.

Artie and Lem remained at the elevator doors, feeling the ship's gravity dissipate. Lem reached forward and grabbed onto Artie's suit.

Artie slammed his fist into the frozen elevator doors as the ice crumbled away. He pressed his gloves in between the door seal, then pried the doors open with his hands.

Looking into the elevator shaft, he could see the long system of tunnels which ran through the center of the ship. The tunnels howled and echoed with the rattle of the ship as it slowed its rotation.

"Good, the elevator shafts weren't breached. Otherwise, you and I would be vacuum dust," said Artie.

"Was this ship ever designed for this purpose?" wondered Lem from behind him.

"Nope," Artie replied floating into the elevator shaft. "That's half the fun. Doing what no one else ever thought possible."

"Clearly," Lem replied.

With a gentle push, Artie drifted down the elevator shaft using the guide rails next to him to steer and slow himself down. Lem floated after him, trying her best not to bump into the side walls creating any noise.

Artie slowed himself down, peering down the next horizontal elevator shaft toward the life support deck. He turned back and stared down to see Lem floating along cautiously behind him. Shoving his foot off the back wall, he drifted down the next shaft at a leisurely speed.

Almost passing the doors to the life support deck, he grabbed hold of the guide rail and stopped himself with a heavy tug. Artie slammed his arm against the glass and tried to pull the doors open. They remained sealed.

"Lem, give me a hand with this," he said down to her.

Lem floated up next to him and pulled back on the other door. The doors ground open as the ice on them broke away.

Looking inside, the floor remained desolate and vacant in the darkness. Lem looked inside, less than excited to go in.

"This is your stop," Artie said to her.

Lem took a deep breath.

She started drifting in when Artie stopped her for a moment. He pointed at the patch on her shoulder. "Rub it for good luck."

Lem glanced down at her patch and rubbed it with her right hand. "Care for some luck?"

"Already had my share, remember? Otherwise, we wouldn't be in this mess," Artie replied with a smile as he drifted up the shaft away from her.

Lem watched him drift away through the door. She turned around and pointed her flashlight across the life support deck, realizing she was now completely alone. She scanned through the shadow-filled corners of the room, working her way over to the life support main terminal.

A yellow light flashed over at the desk, showing that the computer was on and waiting for her. She floated over to it and tucked the flashlight under her arm. The computer screen remained black, but the restart light continued to flash at her. Now all she had to do was wait for Artie to restart the bridge.

Approaching the top, Artie could see the concave corridor leading to the bridge. The ceiling was eerily warped, with remnants of debris still spinning and bouncing around inside. Artie slammed his fist against the door once more, knocking the ice-free before pulling the doors open. He wiggled his way inside, then shut the doors behind him.

Drifting ahead, he ducked and weaved his way beyond the leftover debris toward the bridge. Reaching the airlock to the bridge, he could see the breach in the observation window which stretched from the far port side corner to the very top over the center of the room.

He grabbed the handlebar for the lock, ready to grab the door frame to prevent himself from being blown off into space.

Twisting the lock, the door burst open, giving him no chance to hold on.

Grasping wildly around him, he quickly began floating away toward the breach in the window as the escaping air dragged him along.

Unable to grab hold of anything, the only thought which came to his mind was maybe he really should have rubbed Lem's patch for luck.

Artie suddenly felt a tug on his leg, before coming to a stop and bouncing his shoulder off the port side terminal. He looked down at his feet to see his boot had wedged itself in between the stair railing down to the lower deck and the low wall of the upper deck.

He waited for a moment while the remaining air escaped out through the breach, trying not to move. Hearing nothing but his heavy breaths inside his helmet, he leaned forward from on his back and untangled his foot before grabbing on to the railing.

Cautiously working his way back to his feet, he gazed out across the fractured observation window. Out across a sea of darkness, he spotted their destination. The Earth appeared as a small faint blue star off in the distance away from the sun, now only four days away.

With a gentle push, he glided over to the main console on the bridge, seeing it was partially lit and waiting for his command.

"You ready, Lem?"

"Ready as ever, Cap," Lem replied over the radio.

Artie watched the computer screen flashed and flickered a few times, starting up the reboot sequence. He waited eagerly in his suit until the computer brought up the restart screen, requesting his passcode.

Artie reached out ahead of him and typed in the passcode on the keyboard.

T.S. Wieland

Caitlyn Emilia Glenn

He reflected on the passcode for a moment, then pressed the enter button. The computer flickered once more, then brought up the restart command. Not bothering to wait this time, Artie pressed the restart button and watched as the terminal flickered.

He could feel the subtle vibrations of the ship in his hands holding on to the terminal. He felt a relieving warmth inside. The normal ship commands appeared on the screen, along with a redundant warning about the ship's condition. Artie glanced through all the controls, satisfied to be back in his pilot's seat. At the bottom, right corner of the screen, he noticed the *Camera Feed* button.

He felt hesitant, afraid at what he might see on the recorded videos.

Ready to finally see the face of the killer that they had feared for the past seventeen days, he pressed the button. Artie flipped through the library of feeds back to the day they had left. He started watching all the cameras, knowing almost what time the incident had happened.

Pressing play, he sat stunned by what he was watching, as his heart melted in his chest.

Lem watched as her terminal lit up in the life support cabin. The overhead lights above her pinged and lit up, clearing away the darkness from the room around her. Despite the frost and cold air, she felt warmed by the sight of the ship she had grown to love breathing back to life around her.

The terminal in front of her flashed, requesting if she wanted to restart the life support system. Lem pressed the *yes* button, finding it dumb that the computer would even ask such a question in the first place.

The rounded turbines in the room next to her started to hum and spin back to life. She watched the tank readings start to fade back to normal, letting her know the system was online and working. She grinned with satisfaction.

A small, white and yellow scrap of metal suddenly bounced off her cheek. She picked it out of the air and examined it in her hand. She recognized it as a fragment from the main oxygen line in the room that was black and yellow color coded.

She turned toward the pipes leading away from the oxygen circulation system and drifted over to them to see where it might have come from. One of the safety valves on the forward oxygen line has a junction valve that was now flashing a red warning light at her, indicating the pipe was now closed off from the others. She followed the lineup past the junction, where she noticed another small scrap of the pipe floating in the air.

Lem observed the pipe ahead of her, seeing what looked like another bite taken out of it. She floated over to the marks, immediately recognizing it as the same markings from the broken fuel pipe she and Cliff found on the forward deck.

"You on your way back down Lem?" asked Lara over the radio.

"Yea, on my way now."

Lem continued to stare at the pipe, trying to remember where she had seen markings like that before. Turning around, she could hear the clean air vent in the room trying to suck something in it wasn't supposed to.

She drifted over to the vent and reached her hand. Looking down at her hand, she pulled out an empty cigarette carton.

All at once, she finally realized where she had seen the markings before.

Her broken cutting torch she had loaned to Patrick.

Sixteen

May 27, 2187
– 3 Days, 21 Hours Left –

"You son of a bitch!"

Lem shoved her way past Lara as she reentered the cargo bay, the empty cigarette carton crumpled in her fist. She clawed her way across the across cargo bay and grabbed Patrick by the collar, slamming him into a crate against the back wall.

"The hell's wrong with you!" shouted Patrick pushing her off him.

Lem clasped her hands around his collar more tightly, slamming him back against the crate again, surprising Patrick with how strong she was. "You did this to us!"

Lara rushed over to them and pulled Lem back away from Patrick. Lem spit at him with a deep-seated hatred.

"Jesus, Lem! The hell's wrong!" asked Lara.

Lem brushed Lara's hands away from her furiously. "He's the one who crippled the ship. He's the one who caused all of this!"

"What do you mean, Lem?" asked Cliff.

"That break in the gas line upstairs wasn't that monster. It was you. You used my cutting torch to cut a hole in the ship's forward oxygen line, then tossed one of your cigarettes in trying to blow us all to kingdom come."

Patrick laughed at her. "You think I blew up the ship?"

Lara and Cliff stared at Patrick. An unsettling atmosphere filled the bay.

"I found this empty pack stuck in the vent," said Lem passing the empty pack over to Lara.

Patrick glared at Lem. "I leave those all over the place. And even if that were true, I left the cutter in the engine bay, so there's no way I could have cut a hole in anything."

Cliff took the pack from Lara's hand and examined it. Lara and Cliff stared back and forth between the two of them, unsure who to side with. Lem's conviction was strong, but not strong enough to convince anyone else.

Patrick stood with his arms out in utter disbelief. "You find one of my empty packs upstairs where one of the pipes broke and you think I tried to kill all of us. I'm ashamed of you, kid. I thought you'd be more open-minded than that."

"Wait," Lara interrupted, holding her hand out to Patrick.

She floated over to the door and opened it. She looked both ways down the hallway, keeping an eye out for the creature. She then drifted her way down to the supply closet where she saw Patrick earlier.

Opening the door, she started tossing through everything inside. Everyone followed her out to the closet, watching Lara dig through the cupboards.

"I've already looked in there for another pack of smokes. You're wasting your time," Patrick replied.

Lara scanned the small room, unable to find anything. She suddenly noticed a black charred object resting on the shelf inside.

She moved down closer to the floor and dragged the object out from the back.

It was Lem's cutting torch.

Patrick drifted idly for a moment. With one fluid motion, he laid a punch out across Lem's right eye and pushed off from her. Cliff reached out with his one good arm and grabbed onto the edge of the supply closet before planting his foot into Patrick's chest.

Patrick slammed against the side wall and bounced off with a loud grunt.

Lara hurried out of the closet and together with Lem, shoved him back into the cargo bay door with one unified kick.

Hurrying in after him, Lem moved inside and waited for Lara and Cliff to float back inside before locking the door closed behind them.

"Why Pat?" asked Lara.

Patrick laughed hysterically, reorienting himself. His deranged laughter echoed through the bay. "Why else? I've got nothing left to lose."

Lem grabbed the crate jack near Cliff's sleeping area and held it at the ready, in case Patrick tried anything again.

"Before we left for the station, my wife informed me her new husband pissed away all her money and savings through shit business deals and gambling. After the last deal hit the fan, he left her and my only son to starve with nothing, while he disappeared.

"I could give less of a shit what happened to her when she first came groveling to me about wanting to remarry. I told her I didn't have the money to help, nor would I help her even if I could. Any money I had would go to my son Rye, anyway. A few days after we left, I got a message from him informing me she had overdosed on her own medication.

"I hid in the engine room and drowned my sorrows in a bottle. All her debts got passed on to him, along with the funeral costs. I spent the rest of the trip to the station trying to think of a way to help him since I didn't have the money to help either. Then it occurred to me that in the event of my death, presumably by accident, the company would be obligated to provide my son with a lifetime's worth of compensation, and he could collect on my life insurance policy to pay off the debts and build a better life for himself. One without me or his mother dragging him down.

"So, I turned off the SOT when we got to the station, and let the ship do the rest. Unfortunately, that didn't work out, thanks to you and Artie interfering. So, once we left the station, I figured I'd have to do something more drastic and more believable. I wanted to spare all of you, and myself the pain and suffering, so I had hoped that with the argon, we could have all gone quietly in our sleep. But once again, you all miraculously found out, and my hand was forced to help and try and think of another plan."

"You're suicidal," muttered Lara with a deep scowl.

"My son is the only reason I have to live, Lara. And as a father, I'm willing to give him my life if it helps him. I've spent long enough wandering this solar system, looking for a purpose. Now I think I finally found one," Patrick replied.

Lem grabbed Patrick by the collar once more. Lara rushed over and pulled her away. "You let that thing loose on this ship trying to kill all of us!?"

Patrick glared at her confused. He snickered. "You think I would release that thing on all of us after I went through all the trouble to try and end all our lives peacefully? I never even knew it was onboard. That was just an unexpected result. I haven't even seen it with my own eyes this whole time."

"That's because it doesn't exist," said a voice from behind everyone.

Everyone looked back to see Artie standing in the doorway with his space suit still on, his helmet under his arm. He let go of the helmet and let it drift away.

"What?" asked Cliff.

"How long have you been there?" asked Lem.

"Long enough to know everything," muttered Artie scowling at Patrick.

Artie drifted over toward Lara. He stared into her eyes, still seeing the swirling fear behind them. The paranoia within. "It does. I've seen it!" Lara argued.

"Have you, Lara?" Artie questioned. "Have any of us seen it?"

Cliff thought for a moment. He believed at one point he saw it stalking in the darkness before him, but soon realized he never *actually* saw it clearly with his own two eyes. For all he knew, the shadows could have been playing tricks on him.

Lem stared at the cargo floor, thinking to herself. She thought hard, realizing every time she had come close to witnessing the creature's horrifying appearance, she turned and fled.

"I saw it, Art! I saw it with my own eyes! That's not possible," said Lara with the utmost assurance in her voice.

"I went to the lab in the cargo, Lara. I saw the crate it came in. It was untouched, completely intact. I opened it myself just to see, and all I found inside was a bunch of rock samples. I saw no foot prints. Just bloody boot prints. Your bloody boot prints."

Lara drifted both in mind and body, with a vacant expression.

She couldn't believe what she was hearing, feeling her stomach rise to her throat.

"You killed them, Lara."

She peered into her husband's eyes. "No," Lara immediately replied.

"What?" muttered Lem in confusion.

Cliff drifted over to them. "What about the walls? That creature destroyed the hallway outside!"

"The water pipes leaked into the walls. The ice expanded while the walls didn't. The same reason we had to break through a dam of ice to get to the reserves."

"But we all heard the screams," said Lem.

Artie drifted back over toward the control panel near the door. He tapped on the screen a few times.

"EEEEEEERRRRRR!"

The horrific scream echoed throughout the hallways outside.

Everyone stared at him with doubt.

"It was the air circulation system. We never heard anything while we were dealing with the gas leak because it was off. It ran on and off throughout the last several days, damaged by the hull breach."

Reality began to sink in.

Lem felt a nauseous feeling well up inside her.

Cliff shook his head in disbelief.

Patrick snickered in delusion and madness.

Artie gazed at each of the shattered faces of his crew. "We've been driven by our own paranoia this whole time. Chasing figments of our imaginations."

Artie drifted back over to Lara. He reached out and placed something in her hand. "A figment of your imagination, Lara."

Lara looked down into her hand as Artie moved away. It was her bracelet. The same one she thought she threw away back on the station.

Lara continued to shake, feeling her grasp on reality start to slip into vertigo. She remembered the creature clawing at her in the infirmary. The mark on her ankle. It wasn't from a claw, but from a scalpel off the table.

She thought back to when she was standing at the door to the cargo bay. Her repressed memories began to flood back into her mind.

Artie drifted over to the control panel and pulled up the camera feed which he had tied into the control panels.

A video appeared on the screen of Lara making her way to the rear compartment alone on the day of the accident.

Lara watched, remembering the moment. As she watched herself walk toward the cargo bay door, her vivid, repressed memories returned. She remembered getting into an argument with Pindrazi about needing to move for their safety. He shouted back at her violently. He put a hand on her trying to push her out the door. She grabbed one of the large rock samples off the table and clashed it across the side of his right temple. Both assistants ran over, trying to stop her.

Fueled by an uncontrollable repressed hate and pain-filled rage, she smashed the rock against Rupert's head, knocking him to the floor in a pool of his own blood. Annie reached out to try and stop her, pleading and screaming at her. She turned on her and started choking her.

Trying to push Lara off her, Annie pulled the bracelet off her wrist and collapsed on the floor. Lara stepped away, drained of all emotion. She gazed down at everyone for a moment in utter disbelief at what she had done. She turned around and started making her way back down the hall to the reserve storage, trembling in shock as she left.

Lara watched on the video as she stopped at the door in the reserve storage. She turned around, shaking in her hands, and all at once, her mind erased everything. Her hands stopped shaking. She emptied it all from her mind.

She walked down to the cargo door, staring down at her blood-covered hand with confusion. Everyone watched the video as she fell on the floor in front of the cargo bay in the pool of Rupert's blood, completely oblivious to what she had done just minutes before. She backed away from the bodies on the floor and ran back down the hall where she hid behind the reserve tank.

She stood next to the tank, cowering in fear. Fear of an empty room, with only the screeches from the air circulator fueling her imagination.

Artie stared at his wife. He didn't know her anymore. "Your mind came up with a monster as a way for you to forget what you did."

Lara looked down at the blood-covered hospital bracelet. She held it in her hand, sobbing. She had killed three people, with no knowledge of it, driven by a long built-up tension of hate, desperation, and loss of a life she had been robbed of.

Patrick laughed under his breath at her. "Seems I'm not the only monster here."

Everyone stared at Lara as she sobbed. Artie bowed his head in anguish, as Cliff and Lem continued to watch in shattering doubt, knowing they had nothing to fear now. The monsters onboard their ship had finally been caught.

Seventeen

May 27, 2187
– 3 Days, 14 Hours Left –

    Lem gently draped the last bed sheet over Cernan's body in the conference room of the living quarters. She stopped in the doorway, seeing the nine passengers from the living quarters laid out across the floor, each one covered with a sheet. Knowing she wasn't the cause of the accident, she still held guilt for each one.

    She closed the door to the conference room and turned the lock behind her. Staring in through the window, she pulled hard on the handle lock, breaking it off and sealing what now had become a tomb.

    Lem walked away with a final glance, mourning the loss of those she knew would never return home.

    Artie sat in the mess hall, sipping at a cold bottle of whiskey he had found in one of the passenger cabins. He could still hear Lara's sobs in his ears down the hall as Patrick shouted and pounded his fists against the door in rage.

Lem quietly walked into the mess hall. She closed the door to the living hall, silencing the heart-breaking cries of her once good friends. She turned back, seeing Artie still sitting where he had been for the past several hours. His bottle of whiskey had hardly been touched, with the clear cup he had been sipping at on only half empty.

Lem sat down on the bench across from him. Artie continued to rest with his hand up to his chin, staring off into his own deep space. His fever had finally broken, but his heart was now shattered.

Cliff opened the door and stepped inside, still trying to hold back the surging pain in his collarbone. "Everything's starting to warm up again. I only had to replace a few fuses on this level, but nothing that should affect us. Lem and I can head downstairs in a few and double check on the strain for the more critical systems."

Artie took a sip from his drink, still zoned out, staring at the table.

"Cap?" muttered Lem.

Artie looked over at her.

Lem could see it in his stare. A man with little to nothing left in his mind. One now forced to face choices he never imagined he would ever be obligated to make. For Artie, it was like he had lost his newborn daughter all over again.

"Thanks, Cliff," he mumbled, taking another drink.

Cliff stared down at his captain, realizing it was the first time he had ever thanked him since he stepped on board. He sat down on the table across from him.

Artie grunted and cleared his throat. "When I first watched the footage, I couldn't believe what I saw. I couldn't believe what my eyes were witnessing. I watched the feed more than five times, trying to make sure it was her. I was in so much denial; I forced myself to work my way down there just to see.

"When I got there, I saw it all for myself. Everything still preserved like the day it happened. Then all I felt was anger. Hatred.

But not at her, but myself. I pleaded with God to take it all back. To give me a chance to make things right again.

"Soon I realized, the universe doesn't give second chances."

Artie finished off the last quarter of his glass in one fluid drink. He reached over for the bottle and refilled the glass half way.

"I'm sorry, Cap," murmured Lem softly.

"What are we going to do?" asked Cliff delicately.

Artie stood up from his chair and walked over to the window, looking out across the side of the ship shining in the sun. He could see the small distant speck of the Earth, now more blue and brighter than before. "We stick to our original plan. Slow down the ship with what power we have left. Steer the ship off course, and use the Schooner to slow us down the rest of the way and make it to the docking stations. Then I'll be forced to turn both of them over to the station police."

The lights in the mess hall flashed for a moment before going dark. Cliff sighed and stood up from the table. "Another breaker probably blew from the condensation. I'll be right back."

Cliff hurried out the mess hall doorway and down the hall, leaving Artie and Lem alone for a moment.

"Cap, we don't have to turn her in. We could just tell them Pat was the one responsible for everything."

"He knows Lara is guilty too. I do not doubt if we turn him in, he'll force me to turn her in as well. If there's still half the woman in there I know, she'll turn herself in any way. At least that way, I might be able to find her some help. Maybe get our old life back."

Lem sat quietly as Artie finished his drink by the window. The lights flickered and came back on. Artie took a deep breath. He was ready to confront Pat face to face.

"Come on."

Lem stood up from her place at the table, following Artie back out into the hall as he placed his glass down on the table.

Artie stepped into the hallway and walked over to the living quarters' doorway. Lem stopped for a moment at the door to the quarters, knowing something wasn't right. "Cap…"

Artie looked back at her.

"I closed this door earlier," she said to him.

Artie thought for a second. He ran down the hall to the room they had locked Patrick away in. The door was wide open.

Artie stood for a moment, trying to think of where Patrick might have gone.

He stared at Lem. His eyes filled with horror. "Oh no…"

Lem and Artie took off down the hall toward the elevator as Cliff returned from fixing the tripped breaker.

"What's going on?" asked Cliff.

"Pat's making a run for the Schooner!" Lem shouted back at him hurrying to the elevator.

Artie slid to a halt in front of the elevator. The elevator was descending and had stopped on the second deck below them. Artie rushed over to the maintenance tunnel to the lower level and pried the hatch open.

"The power outage must have unlocked the doors!" Lem shouted following Artie down the tunnel.

Jumping down to the bottom floor, Arite hurried around the corner to the airlock for the docking bay. He could already see Patrick at the door, trying to break the handle off the lock on his side of the door.

Artie shouted through the doorway at him. "Pat! Stop!"

With a heavy tug, Patrick ripped the handle off the door and threw it down on the ground. He pressed the timed door code for the hangar door. He looked at Lem and Artie through the window, a somber expression of guilt on his face. He then turned around with his steel pipe in hand, and ran toward the Schooner, leaving Lem and Artie standing in the window, shouting at him.

Artie tugged at the door lock viciously, trying to get it open before he could get away. "RRRRR! Go grab something to pry this open with from the cargo bay!" Artie yelled back to Lem.

Lem turned around and hurried down the hall, leaving Artie still trying to open the door.

Patrick hopped up into the Schooner and closed the hatch behind him. He started powering up the Schooner still watching Artie yanking at the door to try and get it open.

Lem returned with the crate jack from the cargo bay. Artie took it from her hand and jammed it between the door handle so he could gain more leverage. Lem moved forward next to him and started helping him try and turn the door handle.

The docking bay alarm blared as the bay started to depressurize. The door gradually started to open. The air from the hallway behind them quickly began rushing in through the gap. Artie let go, letting the door reclose. He hurried back to the control panel in the cargo bay and brought up the radio for the Schooner.

Patrick eased the Schooner out into space through the hangar doors and delicately started flying away from the ship.

"Pat, stop! You destroy that Schooner, not only will we all die, but you'll never get to see your son again," shouted Artie into the terminal.

Patrick eased the controls, drifting the Schooner back around toward the ship, ready to make his final suicidal blow against the crippled engines. "I already accepted that a long time ago, Art. I'm sorry, for what it's worth. I tried my best to end it all peacefully. But even as your friend, my son will always come first. I'm sorry."

Artie held onto the console. "Pat! Come back, and we can talk about another way! I can help you!"

"Godspeed, Art," muttered Patrick over the radio. With a heavy swing, Patrick smashed his steel pipe into the controls in front of him. The panel sparked and buzzed then fell quiet.

Cliff hurried down the hall to the cargo bay from the elevator and stopped at the door to take a breath.

"Lara's gone too."

Artie felt a cold chill pass over him.

Patrick laid back in the cockpit chair and closed his eyes, starting to drift back toward the ship. He let go of his steel pipe in his hand and let it drift around the room.

The back hatch of the Schooner slowly crept open. Lara reached out and grabbed the steel pipe out of the air. She clasped it in her right hand and raised it over Patrick's head.

Patrick opened his eyes, seeing her standing right over him.

"Go ahead. Kill me," he muttered to her. "You and I both know we are the only true monsters in this world."

Lara stood over him, quivering.

"No," she replied. "You're the only monster here."

Lara swung down over his head.

The steel pipe smashed against the viewport.

The glass cracked.

They could hear the air in the cabin starting to escape. Patrick closed his eyes, ready to accept his fate.

Lara gazed out the window through the growing cracks, back at the ship, watching it drift away into a sea of stars, feeling her sanity returned.

Artie watched helplessly from the door window to the docking bay. The Schooner flashed, followed by a bright explosion from the crippled spacecraft.

He held his breath.

The explosion faded from his eyes.

Artie sank to his knees.

Lem and Cliff stood behind him, speechless and in disbelief.

Artie bent down on his hands and knees, and wept.

Eighteen

May 29, 2187
– 18 Hours Left –

    Artie continued to sit silently at the door to the docking bay, hoping Lara would suddenly open the door behind him, clearing away his living nightmare.

    Cliff and Lem sat in the mess hall, unable to stir their captain from his coma for three days. The ship now had a new atmosphere, one of sadness and loss - a drastic change from the constant fear and paranoia that had grown on them. Now seeing the Earth growing bigger and brighter in the window, they needed a new plan.

    Both crew members in the mess hall dwelled over the schematics for the ship, trying to think up a way to save not only themselves but the ship as well. Their efforts, however, continued to face an immovable object. The ship only had enough power and fuel to do one of two things: slow them down, though not nearly enough to use the escape pods as they approached the Earth and survive the plummet to the surface; or alter the ship's course just enough to miss the Earth all together, and be lost in space forever in the ship that would become their own final resting place.

"Could we use what's left in the Schooner batteries we have on board?" asked Lem, trying to scrounge for a new plan.

"Wouldn't help much. We'd still be lacking the fuel we need. Besides, we'd still run into the same problem of not having enough hands," Cliff replied, pointing at his arm still hanging in his sling.

Lem was starting to feel helpless. She and Cliff had refused to give up, spending every waking hour trying to think of a plan while their captain remained checked out of his reality down below.

Lem bowed her head in defeat and laid on the table. "We need his help."

Cliff scratched under his arm. "He's just as gone as everyone else. He didn't respond the first two times; I don't expect him to do so the third."

"We're out of options at this point, Cliff. Right now, our only option is to steer the ship off course, and neither you nor I are willing to let that happen unless we run out of time. We still have eighteen hours left, and I'm not willing to let that be our last act unless we only have thirty minutes left."

Cliff stood up and walked toward the door. "All right, not like we have anything better to do."

Approaching the docking bay door, they both could see Artie hadn't moved from his spot on the floor, resting with his back against the wall. He continued to stare down at his feet. Like a corpse, he sat motionless without blinking.

"Cap?" muttered Lem, walking over to him softly.

Artie remained undisturbed.

Lem sat down on the floor in front of him. "Cap?"

Cliff rested his back against the wall and slid along its metallic surface till he reached the floor. "Old man?" said Cliff, seeing if he could usher a response out of him.

Artie's gaze stayed firmly on his feet, slowly taking in each breath.

Lem moved closer to him. "Cap, we need you. We don't have much time left. If we are going to make it home, we are going to need you."

Artie didn't move.

Lem looked over at Cliff, seeking words of encouragement from him.

"Artie... I mean, Captain, you've kept this ship alive and kept all of us alive so far. As much as I wish I knew how to save the three of us, this is your ship, and I'm all out of ideas. I always like to pretend that I'm the hero around other people and take all the glory and attention, but..."

Cliff looked down at his brother's personal device. "You and my brother, Daniel, you guys are the real hero's worth remembering. You guys never do what you do for the glory or attention; you do it for others without hesitation. It's taken me up till now to realize that, and now I'm glad I stepped on board your ship. Because I've never worked with anyone as brave as you, and I'm honored to serve under your command."

Artie continued to sit, with only a subtle flinch in his expression.

"Cap, you haven't lost everyone. You still have us, and if the rest of us make it home, all our efforts won't have gone in vain."

Artie remained a statue, seemingly unmoved and unchanged.

Lem sighed and stood up. She glanced over at Cliff who did the same.

She reached her hand up across to her shoulder. Grabbing the edge of the flight patch on her jacket, she pulled it off with one pull.

"You can have this back," she said to him placing it down at his feet. "You probably need it more than I do."

Cliff and Lem started walking away down the hall, leaving Artie alone once more. Artie stared down at the patch in his lap, seeing the angel spreading its wings rising from the base, the Earth floating elegantly in the background. He opened his hands, seeing his wife's bracelet still resting in his palm.

"I didn't say you were dismissed," muttered Artie's groggy tone down the hall.

Lem stopped and turned back to him, seeing him stare down at his hand.

Artie pushed off from the ground and stood up. He slipped the bracelet into his pocket and picked up the patch from his lap. He walked over to Lem and handed her back the patch. "You know it's rude to look a gift horse in the mouth."

Lem took the patch back from him.

"Felix Culpa," Artie said to her.

"Felix Culpa," Lem replied with a grin.

Artie smiled back at her, feeling compelled to finish what he had already begun. He reached out and offered her a hug. "Thanks, Lem."

Lem stepped back from hugging him and wiped the water away from her eyes. "As I said before, and I'll say it again, sometimes my captain needs a good ass kicking when he starts acting like one."

Artie turned to Cliff. He extended his hand out to him. Cliff reached out and shook his hand.

"Your ego is still bigger than your mouth, but I'm still glad you joined my crew. You're a smart kid. Any captain would be lucky to have you onboard."

Cliff smiled at him. "And you're a stubborn stick in the mud, but you're still one of the bravest men I've ever met."

Artie let go of his hand and looked down at his watch. "All right, we still have eighteen hours. Let's not waste any more of it standing around sharing sentiments."

Returning to the mess hall, Artie looked through the schematics on the table. "Could we try and patch that reserve fuel pipe and use that?" asked Cliff.

"No, those tanks are probably only a quarter full now, and the lines still busted. We need something else," Artie replied. He ran his finger across the schematic, searching through each of the ship's cabins. He rested his hands on the map, struggling for ideas. The Schooner was their best option, and now they were left floating in a vast ocean with no sign of land.

Artie stared down at his right hand. He lifted his hand off the table and saw the cabin hiding under it. "Maybe we are thinking of using the wrong tanks."

Artie hurried away from the table, leaving Cliff and Lem staring at one another confused. They both scurried after him, following him to the forward cargo bay on the very top deck.

Artie opened the door to the top cargo bay. In two long rows, towering fifteen feet tall, was a total of ten steel tanks. "If we can't slow it down one way, we slow it down another way," Artie said to both of them.

"What are these?" asked Cliff.

"The station's oxygen tanks. All the outer stations recycle air. We take the used air back, they purify it back home, and we take the fresh tanks back with us to deliver to the stations in the outer region. All these tanks are pressurized with recycled air from the station," Artie replied.

"How's that going to help?" questioned Cliff.

"Same way we got into this mess and ended up off course in the first place."

"That's never going to work, Cap," Lem replied following him down the row of tanks.

"Why not? You two asked me for a plan. It's either that, or we take our chances in the escape pods where we'll just end up like bugs on a windshield," Artie replied.

Lem was beginning to regret asking Artie for his help. She had hoped he would come up with a more constructive plan, and not one that could end up killing them all a third way.

"Kid, you know how to set up a relay to the bridge?"

Cliff stared at Artie confused and unsure. "Maybe. Why?"

"We are going to slow this dumpster down."

◆ ◆ ◆

Keeping a diligent eye on the time, Lem handed Artie the last recycled food bag filled with his explosive ammonium mixture. Using a roll of duct tape, Artie tapped the bag close to each of the tank nozzles, while Cliff handed him a final small electrical fuse he had filled with water and resealed. Pushing the glass fuse into the bag, Artie looked at the wires connected to the end of the fuse to make sure they were still attached. Adding the finishing touch, Artie reached out to the tank nozzle and gently turned the large handle so the air inside barely had room to escape.

"You sure these fuses will explode?" asked Lem.

"With enough current running through them, yea," Cliff replied.

Artie slid down the ladder of the last tank. "All right, I think that should work. As long as we have them all in the right order."

Lem watched Cliff run back to the relay box he had linked to the control panel inside the cargo bay. The room hissed with the low soft sound of the tanks leaking oxygen. Lem gazed down the aisle feeling even less confident than seventeen hours earlier. "So, please refresh me on how this is going to work?"

"You guys head for the escape pods and wait for me there. I'll use the suit to get back up to the bridge. Once I'm up there, I'll start up what's left of the ship's engines and use what little we have left to start slowing us down. Assuming this all works out as planned, I'll use the bridge console to blow each one of the fuses. The water in the fuses should wet the powder, and start a fire next to the nozzle. The leaking oxygen catches fire and should rupture the tank. Along with blowing up the front end of my ship, this will help slow us down so we can use one of the pods."

"Or kill us all," Lem replied.

Using one hand, Cliff plugged the connection into the relay and hurried over to the control panel. "You should be all set, captain."

Artie looked down at his watch, then hurried over to the window. The Earth was close enough now that he could see it growing with each passing second. "We've got less than twenty minutes. If we are going to do this, now's the time."

Lem and Cliff nodded in agreement with him. "We'll be waiting for you at the escape pods."

"I'll be there," Artie replied.

Cliff nudged Lem on the shoulder, then hurried out the cargo door. Lem gave Artie a final good luck, then hurried after Cliff, leaving Artie alone in the cargo bay.

Artie stared at all the wired tanks before him, reassuring himself of his plan. "One more hurdle."

♦ ♦ ♦

Reaching the top floor of the elevator, Artie held on to the door handle in the elevator wearing his space suit, ready this time for the air in the elevator to try and drag him out again. The doors in the elevator opened. The sound around him faded to a chilling silence and the sound of his breath in the helmet. He slowly stepped out into the remaining hallwa, and worked his way down the destroyed walkway to the bridge. Stepping out into the sun, he flipped his sun visor down, and carefully climbed his way over to the control panel.

Artie loosened the safety harness straps on his captain's chair to fit around his space suit, then sat down and fastened them around his chest.

He glanced over at Lara's empty seat, knowing it would be the first time, as well as the last time he would ever pilot the ship without her at his side.

"Cap! You ready?" said Lem over the radio.

Lem finished snapping the safety harness around Cliff. Cliff grunted uncomfortably, feeling the harness rub along his collar.

"Sorry. I know this probably won't be the most comfortable ride for you," she said to him.

"I'll probably pass out, so just wake me when we get there," Cliff replied.

Lem sat down in her seat and clicked the harness around her chest, leaving the seat in between her and Cliff open for Artie to hurry in and sit down before they jettisoned from the ship. The door to the escape pod remained open, waiting for its final passenger. "You ready, Cap?"

"Yea. I'm ready," Artie replied.

Artie pulled up the controls on the computer screen in front of him. All the tanks' numbers were lined up on his screen. He took a deep breath, knowing once the first explosion had begun, there would be no turning back.

Artie stared at the screen, seeing the ship's communications were still receiving messages. He reached out and patched the transmission into his helmet.

"Space vessel DATO Six, this is Earth Station Eleven. Do you copy? Over," said a voice over the radio.

Artie felt relieved to hear another human voice.

"Earth Station Eleven, this is DATO Six. We copy you, over," he replied into his helmet.

The computer flashed with an error message.

T.S. Wieland

Failure: Partial Transmission Sent

Artie shrugged in his suit. "Well, was worth a shot. Sorry Station Eleven in advance."

Artie turned off the transmitter and opened his radio to Lem and Cliff. "You guys ready back there?"

"Ready," Lem replied, seeing Cliff give her a head nod.

Artie took one last long, deep breath in his helmet. He disengaged the ship's rotation, watching the Earth settle in plain view before him.

"Three."

He queued up the ship's starting controls.

"Two"

Artie reached up to his chest, feeling Lara's bracelet still in his suit pocket.

"One."

Artie reached out in front of him and started up the ship's engines. The ship trembled around him. Wasting no time, he eased back on the controls, immediately feeling the ship gradually starting to slow around him.

"Brace yourselves, kids," Artie muttered pushing the first two buttons on the panel.

The relay box down in the cargo bay surged. The first two fuses at the forward tanks gave a subtle pop. The powder inside the bag slowly became wet. Artie waited patiently on the bridge.

Two seconds passed.

The powder finally burst into flames in bright showers of orange sparks. With a silent explosion ahead of him, Artie watched the front of his ship light up and erupt into flames.

Lem and Cliff could hear the explosion above them as the pod shook all around them. The ship instantly started to slow down, as all three of them felt as though they were about to be ripped from their seats.

Artie watched the debris all at once rush toward him. The larger reaming piece of the observation deck flew across the deck behind him and smashed against the back wall

Cliff shouted in pain feeling the straps on his collar tug at his neck.

Lem's head flew sideways. Her heart started to race with a new sensation of terror.

The ship gradually released its pull on them. Artie reached out once again and fired the next two tanks.

A moment of silence passed, followed by another explosion and shudder from the ship, and Artie experienced the gripping sensation of being pulled from his seat. He braced himself on his console, trying to relieve the strain on himself while waiting for the remaining air to finish escaping.

"You guys still with me?" shouted Artie into his helmet, watching the Earth grow frighteningly fast in his view.

Lem peered over at Cliff. He was unconscious, swaying in his seat. "We're still here, Cap! Cliff's out cold, but we're still here!"

Artie reached out and pushed the next series of buttons. Another explosion erupted from the bow of the ship. Artie could feel the straps on his seat starting to give way. He struggled to breathe.

The ship continued to slow down. He held onto the console, trying not to let his helmet slam against the panel in front of him.

Lem held firmly on to the handles next to her, feeling her palms sweat. She fought back against the forces bearing down on her heavy heart with each tormented breath.

Artie fired another pair of canisters, feeling ready for it all to end.

His ship gradually began to release its grip on him again. "Last one," he shouted into his microphone.

Artie pressed the last two buttons on the panel.

He stared out through the flames. His ship was on a collision course with a station, and there was nothing he could do to stop it.

He prayed that everyone had quickly gathered, he could not control the ship and had already been evacuated.

The final explosion faded around the nose of the ship.

"That's the last one! Hurry, Cap!" Lem shouted over the radio.

Artie reached out and pulled up the escape pod functions on his screen.

Lem watched as the door to the escape pod gradually started to close.

"Cap!?"

"A captain always goes down with his ship, Lem. You and I both knew there was no way I could make it down there in time. Besides, she's a flying dumpster, but she's my flying dumpster."

Lem tried to reach out and get to the door controls. The straps held her into her seat, preventing her from disarming the door. "We're not leaving you here, Cap!"

"I'm not going anywhere! I'm going home, Lem. Same as you," Artie replied over the radio.

Lem sat back in her seat. "Cap… Artie, please!"

"I know you'll make a great captain one day, Lem."

Lem's eye began to water.

"Tell Cliff to watch his attitude with his next captain, and thank you."

Artie reached out and pressed the ejection button for the escape pod.

Lem eased back in her seat and grabbed hold of the handles again.

"Goodbye, Cap."

The pod burst back from the ship. Lem held on, filled with sorrow.

Artie watched as the pod drifted away from the ship and narrowly pass another station before making its way down to Earth.

He gazed back out in front of him, seeing the station before him speeding toward him with each passing millisecond.

    He reached into his suit pocket and pulled out Lara's bracelet. He held it firmly in his hand, feeling Lara's welcoming touch holding his hand. He was ready to be with her. Together again, traveling across the stars.

    Lem watched out the window as the ship collided with the station before continuing to plummet toward the Earth. The orange ionized air started to build, obscuring her vision just as they made their way toward home. She sat back in her seat and closed her eyes.

Nineteen

June 1, 2187
– Skyliner Hotel –
Orlinia, Carolina

"And you swear that's what happened?"

"Every word."

Cliff and Lem remained firm at their place across the conference table from the DATO executive, Mr. Hidinger. The sound of the news reporters gathering outside could be heard throughout the small office building. Cliff slouched in his chair, holding the bottle of pain relievers the doctors had given him in his hand. Lem continued to stare at the table, still feeling the movement of the ship beneath her.

Hidinger sighed and wrote down the final statements in his folder. He placed the pen down on the paper and sat back in his chair. He let out a heavy sigh of heartache.

"Seems only yesterday I was speaking with Mr. Glenn in the same position you two are in now," muttered Hidinger. "I only wish I were speaking to you under better circumstances."

Lem and Cliff remained silent, wishing not to further discuss their story.

"I hope you both understand you must remain quiet about this whole incident," said Hidinger.

Cliff glared up at him. "Quiet?"

"DATO is a major establishment in our modern economy. Such incidents would only cripple the company even further during these troubling times," Hidinger replied.

Cliff snickered in disbelief. "I don't believe it. You want us to stay quiet so you all can continue sitting on your high castle of profits? Our friends died out there because of company negligence. Not only to their needs but to their mental needs. None of this would have happened if you hadn't turned a blind eye to their basic human rights!"

"Mr. Bore, I can assure you, I will personally file a case considering the matter of both crew safety and mental wellness with the company right away. You have my word on it."

"You mean the same word you gave Art-… Captain Glenn?" muttered Lem. "The same word that forced his hand in the first place? The same word that led fifteen people to their deaths?"

Hidinger remained silent. He rubbed his forehead in hesitation.

"And what if we refuse?" wondered Cliff.

"You'll be prosecuted," Hidinger replied.

Cliff laughed to himself as he sat back in his seat. "Good luck winning that case."

"Miss Duke, Mr. Bore, I give you my wo-… I promise I'll do whatever I can to make this right. Not only for you two, but to Mr. Glenn, and his family. But I would need your word not to speak a word of this to the public."

Lem leaned forward in her seat. "I think I have an idea."

T.S. Wieland

Twenty

December 1, 2188
- Orlinia Central Park -

The endless sounds of city life bounced around the trees of the city park. Lem stood at the monument before her, holding a small cup of ice cream in her hand, enjoying the cold breeze.

"The guy at the ice cream store told me all he had was vanilla today, so I'm hoping that one was your favorite."

Lem gazed down at the black stone engraved memorial at the center of the park, engraved with the patch on her jacket.

In Honor, Love, and Memory of the Crew and Passengers of the Space Vessel, DATO Six
Captain Artie Glenn
First Officer Lara Glenn
First Engineer Patrick Collins

Lem ate another spoonful of her ice cream. "I won't be back this way for a while, so I wanted to say goodbye to you guys before I lost the chance. You wouldn't believe how hard it is to find ice cream in this city during December."

"You ready to go, sweet cheeks? We're set to take off in four hours, and I don't think the station shuttle is going to wait for us," said Cliff walking toward her.

"That ship's not going anywhere without its captain. I'm almost ready," Lem replied looking over at him.

She reached across her chest and rubbed the patch on her shoulder, then stepped forward to place her hand on the memorial.

Cliff watched her rest her palm on the snowy site of remembrance, as she shared the luck from her patch just as always before they began another long journey across deep space. He stepped forward and did the same.

They both stepped back and shared a moment of silence. Lem closed her eyes, sensing the love of her only family still with her, always at her side.

Lem opened her eyes again. "Now… Now I'm ready."

Believe what you want to believe you've heard. Crazed captain crashes his ship into the Indian Ocean. Crippled DATO vessel nearly kills an entire station. DATO ship abandoned after takeoff by the crew. But, despite how hard they try, no matter how much they pay, Cliff and I will always know what really happened during those twenty-six days.

We never told them about Patrick, allowing his son to inherit the payments for his loss. Nor did we ever tell them what really happened to Lara. As far as we know, in the public's eye, they both died alongside the other passengers. But so long as Cliff and I are alive, people will know the tale of DATO Six. How the only monsters we should fear are our own. How Artie Glenn became the name known across every station for his courage. And no matter how dim and dark life gets, there's always a shimmer of hope somewhere, with some good that can come of it.

Humans will always find a way to survive, even when we seem destined to fail. We go out fighting and are willing to make sacrifices if necessary. Because when the odds are against us, that's when we rise to the occasion and always find a way to turn them back in our favor. Because true heroes never know when to quit.

Felix Culpa.

Read more thrilling and adventurous novels by T.S. Wieland at
www.TSWieland.com

The Space Foundation builds awareness of the benefits of space through our Space Certification™ program, which demonstrates how space technologies improve life on Earth and makes space more interesting and accessible to everyone.

Products and services that display the Space Certification seal are guaranteed to have stemmed from or been dramatically improved by technologies originally developed for space exploration or to have significant impact in teaching people about the value of space utilization.